THE STAG

Clan Ross of the Hebrides Novella

Pink Door Publishing

ISBN: 978-1-939356-95-6

Also By Hildie McQueen

Clan Ross of the Hebrides

The Lion: Darach

The Beast: Duncan

The Eagle: Stuart

The Fox: Caelan

The Stag: Artair

Clan Ross Series

A Heartless Laird

A Hardened Warrior

A Hellish Highlander

A Flawed Scotsman

A Fearless Rebel

A Fierce Archer

Moriag Series

Beauty and the Highlander

The Lass and the Laird

Lady and the Scot

The Laird's Daughter

Clan Ross of the Hebrides

This fictional story takes place at the beginning of the 17th century in the Scottish Hebrides, isles off the Isle of Skye's western coasts.

In the 1500s, lordship over the Hebrides collapsed and the power was given to clan chiefs. The MacNeil, in Barra; The Macdonald (Clanranald), in South Uist; The Uisdein, in North Uist; and The MacLeod, the isles of Harris and Lewis.

For this series, I have moved the clans around a bit to help the story work better. The clans' locations in my books are as follows. The MacNeil will remain in Barra. The Macdonald (Clanranald) is moved to North Uist. The Uisdein resides in Benbecula. The MacLeod remains in the Isles of Harris and Lewis. My fictional clan, Clan Ross, will laird over South Uist.

CHAPTER ONE

Spring 1603

Artair Ross leaned forward, his elbows on the table as he listened to his father talk about what happened with the people in the surrounding lands. By contrast, across from him, his younger brother Bryce sat back with his arms crossed, a sullen expression of boredom.

Despite his recent ailments, their father was robust and full of energy as he spoke, his voice strong to ensure they listened.

"Both of ye will follow in my footsteps. We have farmland and families who depend on us."

His hazel gaze moved from Artair to Bryce. "As of late, both of ye have barely been in the same room together. I need to know ye are going to be united once I am gone."

At the last words, Bryce straightened. "Ye should stop speaking as if ye're on yer deathbed Da. Ye are not."

Their father's right eyebrow hitched. "A month ago, I almost died. It made me realize there is much that needs to be done to ensure ye and yer brother can take over the family responsibilities."

"Da," Artair began, "ye have taught us all we need to know. We are well aware of what our duties are."

"Is that so?" Angus Ross gave him a pointed look. "Tell me which farmer is having trouble with blight having overtaken his crops. Which family requires help with building a stronger stable because they have added more cows?"

"McConnell has the most livestock," Bryce replied with a triumphant look in Artair's direction. "I rode past Burton's lands the other day. His plantings were brown."

Angus shook his head and let out a sigh. "McConnell died two years ago. Burton is no longer farming. He and his wife went to Bara to live with their son."

How had he missed so much? Artair glared at his brother.

Artair kept eye contact with Bryce. "Ye have been here the entire time. There is no excuse for ye not to know these things."

Artair then spoke to his father. "I work for the laird, ye are aware my duties have taken me from here for the last twenty years. And though I may not be aware of what goes on, I have always made it a point to come here every fortnight or so to ensure ye are well."

"I am not pointing fault at either of ye," their father assured them. "What I wish to point out is that neither of ye are informed well of what happens around here. If I died tomorrow, yer mother and the families depending on us would need one, if not both of ye present and able to take charge."

The brothers exchanged looks and immediately Artair knew his brother had no intention of taking responsibility. Bryce preferred a life of leisure, passing each day doing as little as possible. He rarely did anything more strenuous than lift a quill and spent his days with his nose in a piece of parchment writing.

For years Artair's father and brother had fought over Bryce's lack of interest in the obligations that would one day fall upon him, but despite any threats or demands made by their father, their mother always came to Bryce's defense. Bryce was coddled and refused to change.

"I will ask Darach to reassign me to the southern post," Artair said, referring to his cousin and laird, Darach Ross. "It will enable me to come home more often and spend time with ye. Living closer will also afford me the opportunity to fulfil both my duties."

His father brightened. "That is a splendid idea."

Both looked to Bryce, who'd resumed his previous position and expression of disinterest. He let out a long sigh. "I believe to have gotten Isla Quinn with child. I have to consider what to do."

Artair couldn't hold back the bark of laughter. "How did ye manage that much energy?"

Despite the stern look, he could see the humor in his father's eyes. "Ye will do right by the lass and marry her."

"Marry?" Bryce sat up straight as a rod. "Marry her?"

"That is what I said. Yer mother will invite the family for a meal to formally announce the engagement. I urge ye to go in search of the lass and inform her immediately."

His father's direct gaze left no room for argument. "Do not defy me on this. Ye will have to take responsibility for your actions and perhaps this will make ye grow up."

"Of course, ye will use this as an opportunity to make me serve ye. There is absolutely nothing that interests me about farming . . . or goats."

Tired of his brother's laziness, Artair rounded the table and grabbed Bryce's tunic, hauling him to his feet. "What do ye intend to do? Have a bastard-born bairn running about while ye spend yer life doing nothing more than picking flowers?"

Bryce shoved him back. "Ye know nothing." He stormed from the room.

"What did he mean by that?" Artair asked.

"He claims to feel the need to write and do nothing else," their father replied, looking in the direction his youngest son had gone. "Yer brother refuses to grow up. Perhaps ye should take him with ye on yer next guard duty. He needs to experience more than being a pampered idiot."

By last meal, Bryce acted as if all was well. Their mother spoke at length about the spring festival in the village she was helping with. Along with her companion, Bettina, she spent most days riding back and forth to the village meeting with other women making plans for whatever event was on the horizon. It kept her occupied and, from her bright smile as she spoke, happy.

"I am so glad ye will be spending more time home. I worry about yer da. He needs to rest more." His mother's bright face was endearing, while at the same time, he wondered why she did not demand more from her other son.

Artair bit his tongue to keep from pointing out that Bryce lived there and should have been made to help. Instead, he slid a look to his brother, who ate with gusto, seeming to have forgotten the earlier discussion.

"Mother, I am going to be working at the southern post, which is less than half a day's ride from here. I will let Darach know I will be dividing my time between my duties as guard and here. I am sure he will have no problem with allowing it."

"Why are ye asking him for permission?" Bryce asked, a

bitter edge to the words. "He is father's nephew, therefore, anything to do with Da should be done without having to bow down to Darach."

It took a great deal of strength to keep from yanking his brother across the table again. "Because I have declared my loyalty to his station as Laird of our clan, Bryce."

Like a petulant lad, Bryce rolled his eyes.

"I am also asking that ye be allowed to join the guard for a while. Ye will come with me to help with protecting the southern shore. It will make it easier for me to leave and come here."

Bryce choked on his food and coughed until his face turned a bright red. A tendril of satisfaction traveled through Artair.

"A guard?" their mother asked, then stopped speaking when her husband gave her a stern look.

"Aye Iona," his father said. "I think it will be good for our son to see what it is like to protect one's home."

"What about the Quinns?" Bryce finally managed to sputter. "I thought we were to have them for a meal."

"The Quinns?" their mother asked looking from the still red-faced Bryce to her husband. "What about the Quinns?"

Angus waved his hand dismissively. "Bryce thinks to have gotten Isla Quinn with child."

The incredulous look on their mother's face was what Artair figured his own had been like. "When did this happen?"

Bryce shrugged. "We have been meeting for a few months. She only discovered it recently."

"We must speak to her parents immediately." Their mother glared at Bryce. "It best not be true, or I will pull every hair out of yer head. Isla is a sweet girl. How could ye Bryce?"

When her eyes became shiny with unshed tears, Artair felt bad. Their mother had always been overly sensitive.

"There, there, Iona," their father said in a gruff voice. He hated seeing his wife upset. "I am sure this will all work itself out."

TWO DAYS LATER, both families sat at the same table in uncomfortable stilted silence. As his mother described, Isla was pretty and sweet—and obviously mortified. Her father was enraged. Her mother embarrassed.

To Artair's shock, Bryce took full responsibility and barely flinched when her father threatened to kill him.

The wedding would be within a fortnight to ensure Isla's extended family would not suspect the pregnancy.

After the meal, Bryce strolled into the study where Artair and his father looked over the ledgers.

"I suppose this means I must remain behind and ensure all is well with my bride."

Their father stood. He rounded the table and shoved Bryce backward. He fell into a chair and looked up at their father, wide-eyed.

"Ye will go with yer brother. Ye will return for the wedding. Remain three days and then go back to yer duties at the southern post. This does not give ye any kind of reprieve, but instead makes it doubly important that ye do something to make yer wife and bairn proud."

Artair groaned. The last thing he wanted along at the moment was his annoying and unskilled brother. The southern post was currently one of the most dangerous assignments.

His duties and life had just become much too complicated.

CHAPTER TWO

THE FOOD AT the southern post were flavorful. The cook, Alpena, took pride in feeding the men and took great care with each meal.

Men came and went, assured that upon arriving they would be fed well. Artair glanced from his food to the other end of the table where Bryce sat. His brother was telling an exaggerated story of fighting off a wolf, which made the men laugh. If nothing else, his brother knew how to entertain people.

A warrior walked through the doors and straight to where he sat.

"One of the guards, John, is dead. The other barely survived," Struan McLean, a Clan Ross warrior, reported. The muscular man rolled his shoulders in frustration. "I do not know how the attackers got past us."

Another pair of men hurried in with a man on a makeshift stretcher. Immediately he was seen to by one of the women who worked in the kitchen and had knowledge of healing.

The man was unconscious, which was good as his injuries would bring great pain upon his coming to.

"We must go at once," Artair announced looking to the others. "Who wishes to go?

THEY RODE FROM their quarters in Taernsby past the tiny fishing village, following nearly indistinguishable horse tracks. The men they sought were obviously experienced at hiding by their ability to not leave a consistent trail.

"They must be camped out in the forest." Artair inhaled the salty air while scanning the surroundings. "We must find them and make them pay," he said, his tone dripping with rage.

The guards had been attacked without provocation, according to the one who'd survived. It meant whoever did it was either mad or had a death wish. They had to be aware Clan Ross had a huge army and that they'd be tracked down and punished.

"I'll go west, past the forest. Ye and ye come with me," he said motioning to men and then looked to the four who awaited instructions. Among them Bryce, who looked to be in pain.

After the ride from his parent's land, Bryce was not prepared for another full day on horseback. He met Artair's attention with a bland look.

"Ye four go in that direction," he said pointing to a hill. "Be with care as ye find a way to go up the hill. We do not know what we are up against."

Looking to Bryce, he added. "Keep my brother alive." His lips twitched. "If ye can."

"I can always ride back to the guard post," Bryce replied with a sneer. "This is an utter waste of time."

The guards gave Artair a look saying they'd prefer if he'd do just that.

"Do not try me in this brother," he snapped, and Bryce

looked up at the sky.

IN THE SHADOWS of the forest, the sun's rays broke through the trees sporadically, offering only a small bit of warmth. To fight the chill in the air, Artair and his companions wrapped their tartans around their shoulders as they took their time climbing through the dense hilly area. They stopped often to study the surroundings to ensure they did not miss any signs of which way the men were headed. It was painstakingly slow progress, but experience taught him it was an effective way to track.

His horse, a black beauty named Hagar, trotted down the path with ease. Like him, the animal did not take kindly to remaining in one place for too long. Preferring instead to be led toward unfamiliar territory and unknown lands. The beast snorted and bobbed its head, a sign it heard something or sensed danger.

Holding up a hand, Artair signaled for the others to stop.

Taking in the surroundings, Artair realized how different the area was from the opposite shore. The area there was untamed and wild, patches of trees and vegetation which made for plenty of places for both men and beasts to hide.

"What do ye think?" he asked Struan, who studied the ground.

"New path there." The man pointed to their left. "Old path there." He motioned directly ahead.

Eric Larsen, a master tracker and someone Artair trusted without reservation, rode up and dismounted. The man walked to the new path, kneeled, and touched the ground. Then he looked up to the trees as he walked back to the waiting warriors. "A group of men on horseback rode through here. At least six horses."

The Norseman had arrived several years earlier, asking for work. The late laird had eagerly accepted, claiming to need someone who spoke the language for whenever he decided to fight the Norse. No one had ever heard Erik speak Norse, so Artair doubted he did.

Despite having to fight to be accepted, after a few months, Erik became an integral part of the laird's guard. He'd proven to be a brave warrior and extremely loyal to the clan.

"I think we need to return to the village and gather more men before continuing our search," Struan said, his dark gaze narrowing.

"I agree," Artair said while scanning the surroundings. "Hopefully, they will consider themselves safe and remain close by." It would be dangerous to go farther without being aware of how many attackers there were.

Turning the horses around, they rode back in the direction they came. As they approached the outskirts of the village, Erik rode off toward the guardhouse to gather additional men, Artair and Struan headed to the village to see if they could find anything that might lead them to the men they were searching for.

Taernsby was picturesque. Like most seaside villages, cottages lined the higher ground with smaller shacks closer to the water. Boats bobbed on the water from which fishermen tossed nets.

The two men rode down the center of the village until reaching the square and then dismounted and tied their horses. Artair, his gaze flat, looked for any signs of men who looked to not fit in. It was early yet in the day, so there were plenty of people about. He neared a stand where a couple were roasting meat and waited patiently for them to serve several in front of him.

When it was his turn, he asked for two orders of roasted lamb and flat bread, then went to sit on a nearby bench to eat. Struan came and sat next to him, and both downed their food, hungry from the excursion.

"Where do ye plan to settle?" Artair asked the man who'd recently moved to the Isle since leaving his home on Skye.

Struan shrugged. "I have no plans other than to remain in service to the laird and perhaps, over time, come to a place like this and decide to remain."

"Not for some time, I gather?" Artair wasn't sure why he asked, other than his father's request weighed heavy on his mind. He'd not considered that upon his father's death he would be tied to the land and house there. For whatever reason, he'd grown more restless over time, the opposite of where he should be mentally.

"No not for some time," Struan replied and gave him a curious look.

"Ye?" Struan asked, his gaze returning to scanning the surroundings.

"My father expects I will live at our family home, on family lands." It was not an answer, more a statement of what his future held. Certainly, he had no choice but to honor his father's request.

"Ah, family," Struan said. "Interesting how they plan for us to do as they did, expecting we should want the same."

"My father was quite ill recently. I suppose it made him consider what he wishes and requires of me."

His friend nodded in understanding. "I am going to the tavern. When men travel through a village, most end up at the tavern," Struan said.

"Ask for two rooms," Artair called out as the sun would set soon and he did not expect them to head back out to search with the larger number of guards until the following morning.

They headed in opposite directions. Artair stowed the horses for the night and spoke to the stable master who claimed to have seen several new faces of late. The man narrowed his eyes in the direction of the hillside where Artair had been. "My wife saw them and immediately knew they are harbingers of death."

"We will find them," Artair said, and the man nodded.

The man gave a firm nod. "Good."

Upon returning in the direction he'd come, Artair took a moment to decide where to go next. Just then a young boy sprinted to the same stand where Artair had purchased his meal, grabbed a huge piece of meat, and raced away. The couple didn't notice they'd been robbed and remained talking to a man who was making a purchase.

Artair followed after the boy. Quick as a hare, the lad hurried past several buildings before darting between two. Following at a distance, Artair noted that the boy didn't bother looking back, instead, he slowed as he arrived at a cottage.

The lad had to be held responsible for what he did.

Yes, the boy was still young and perhaps having fun. However, he would grow up stealing if allowed to get away with it.

Artair neared the cottage, alert to his surroundings. The last thing he needed was for someone to attack while he was on a silly quest of chasing a wayward lad.

It was quiet, the only sounds the twitter of birds in the nearby trees. Even as he approached the door, he realized there were no voices or sounds coming from inside.

Artair went to a window and peered in through the slats of the shutter. The boy sat at a table, carefully cutting the meat. He then placed some on a plate and covered it with a cloth. The interior was clean and tidy.

The boy looked familiar, a memory struck, and he narrowed his eyes. He knew this boy.

Now that he considered it, the boy's clothes were well-made and clean, which should be an indicator that he was not so poor that he had to steal for his meals.

Unless . . . the boy lived alone.

Artair turned away, not sure what to do next. He had more important things to worry about at the moment. He would stop by the next day and speak to the boy and his parents. Whatever the situation was, the clan would help.

"What are ye doing?"

A woman's voice startled him. So much for staying alert.

Artair whirled around and came face to face with a young brunette. She was perhaps ten years younger than his six and thirty, very pretty and had the wary look of a wild doe caught by surprise. Her wide, expressive brown eyes looked over him, lingering on his right shoulder, where the hilt of his sword was visible.

She held a basket filled with vegetables in one hand and in the other, two fish on a string. Her gaze flitted to the front door.

"Go away, please." This time her voice shook with what he thought was either nervousness or fear. "We do not have anything for ye to take."

Artair let out a grunt. "*I* am not the thief."

Once again, her eyes widened, and she looked to the door. "Oh no. Please. I will pay ye for whatever he took."

"He took roasted lamb from the village square." Artair stopped talking, trying to reconstruct his sentence better.

"Ye sell lamb?" She looked over her shoulder. "What happened to the Millers?"

"I do not sell lamb. I was eating it."

"He took yer lamb?" Her shoulders fell, but at the same time, she did not relax. "Please take these." She held out the fish. "I am so sorry. He must have gotten hungry waiting for me."

Why was he doing such a horrible job of explaining himself? Artair pressed his lips together. "Ye do not remember me then? Perhaps because I am wearing clothes and not astride my horse."

If possible, her eyes widened further. There was a flicker of recognition. Her cheeks reddened and she took a step back. "Oh dear."

"Yer boy is a menace. First, he steals my clothes and now he takes food from unsuspecting people. Ye must punish him."

Several months earlier while on patrol, Artair had decided to soak in the chilled waters of a nearby loch. His right leg had been bothering him and the cold water seemed to help.

While bathing, the same boy had stolen his clothes. In the end he'd had to ride after him, fully nude, to demand his clothes back. It had been the first time he'd met the dark-haired beauty, whom he'd not forgotten.

Obviously, he'd not made as much of an impression.

She put the basket down and plopped the fish atop the vegetables. There was a spark of something akin challenge in her eyes when she looked at him. "What would ye have me do? Draw and quarter him? He is an energetic boy. Aye. But also a good one. I will speak to the Millers." Her hands formed fists as if she was ready to do hand-to-hand battle.

Artair gave her a droll look. "I will return. This matter is not over. Right now, I have more important things to do."

"Obviously ye do not." She hitched her chin and glared at him.

"It is not safe for ye to be out here alone. Ye should ensure yer husband accompanies ye back and forth to the village. A pair of my guardsmen were attacked recently."

With her basket in hand, she gave him a subtle nod and walked toward the front of the cottage giving him a wide berth. "I shall be careful."

CHAPTER THREE

ROBENA MACKAY HURRIED inside and bolted the door behind, then, placing the basket on the floor, hurried to the window. The man walked away. His gait was strong and assured. The huge sword strapped to his back a clear giveaway that he was a warrior.

He'd not told her his name, and after meeting him for the second time—both under bad circumstances—she wasn't sure she wanted to know it.

"Ye took food from the Millers." She made a point to look at her son directly. "Why?"

Finn was a smart lad. But he was wily, always up to some mischief or another. However, he was also quick to help others. Unfortunately, he loved the challenge of taking things without being caught.

"Come along." Robena motioned to the door.

The boy's eyes widened. "Where are we going?"

"To speak to the Millers. Ye will tell them what ye did and offer to repay."

"I have no coin. Neither do ye."

She pushed him gently toward the door and they went out. "And yet I find a way to bring food home and ensure we have all we need. I work and offer to do tasks in exchange."

Ignoring her growling stomach, she walked to the village,

her sulking son seeming to walk slower and slower until she took his arm.

"I am hungry and tired. I've spent the day working. I am not in the mood for ye to act like this."

The Millers were understanding and upon Robena insisting Finn repay them with work, they asked that he return the following day and work at their stand. Finn became excited at the idea of it, a wide grin stretching across his face.

A familiar figure appeared and Robena's stomach tightened. The older woman's cold gaze traveled over her then flitted to Finn—and instantly softened.

"Why have ye not brought Finn to visit?" the woman asked. "I have every right to spend time with my grandson."

Robena had never understood why her mother-in-law hated her. For years she'd done her best to ingratiate herself with the woman. But, like her deceased husband, the woman been sternly against any kind of interaction that did not involve pointing out everything Robena did wrong.

"I will bring him when I have time away from my duties," Robena said, taking Finn's hand. "We best go."

"He could come with me now. I am going to meet with the constable and his wife." Elena Mackay gave her a pointed look. "I am to speak to them about ye as a matter of fact."

At the words, Robena's breath caught. It was not the first time the woman had tried to take her son away. In Elena Mackay's estimation, after the death of her own son, Robena owed her a replacement.

That the accident, the overturning of a bìrlinn, was not any of her doing, didn't seem to matter. The woman acted as if Robena had caused the storm that day.

There was hatred in her hardened expression meeting Robena's gaze. "This would be so much easier. Ye know the boy wishes to live with me."

Both she and Elena turned to Finn, who'd lost interest and was throwing small pebbles toward a puddle.

"He is my son and will remain with me. The reason I do not bring him to visit is because of yer threats. I do not trust ye." Robena turned and grabbed Finn's hand to lead him away. The boy whirled toward his grandmother and threw his arms around the older woman's waist.

It was true, her son did love the woman. He didn't see her hard stares, or the hatred whenever she looked at Robena. Now, as Elena met her gaze with a triumphant one, Robena fought not to tear her son from the woman's arms.

"Come along Finn," she said instead.

Elena Mackay held him just a bit longer, whispering things into the boy's ears. Finally, Finn extricated himself and went to Robena.

"What did she tell ye?" Robena asked, pretending to not be bothered. "What did yer grandmother promise ye this time?"

"She said I can come live with her and grandfather and that I could learn to shoot with a bow and arrow," Finn explained with excitement. "And she said her cook would make me sweet tarts."

Her heart broke that Finn apparently did not realize the invitation was not extended to her. "I would not be able to come and live with ye," Robena explained. "Would ye not be sad about it?"

Finn's skinny shoulder lifted and lowered. "I suppose. But ye can visit."

In truth, the entire time she'd been married, her husband's family had kept Finn from her, barely allowing Finn to spend more than a few hours here and there with her and her family. The boy had gone on long trips, sometimes months on end with his father. When he'd returned, it was as if they were strangers. It was probable Finn saw her as more of a care giver, not a mother figure.

"DO YE LOVE me, Finn?" Robena asked that night at she helped him to bed. She pushed his hair aside and kissed his forehead. "Because I love ye dearly."

The boy smiled. "I do. Ye are my mum."

The words melted her heart despite knowing her son would much prefer to be with the Mackay's than with her.

Closing the door to her old bedroom, Robena walked down the short hall to what used to be her parent's bedchamber. Instead of going to the bed, she went to the window to peer out at the night sky. It was her favorite thing to do, to dream of simpler days. It had been a horrible mistake to fall in love with a man she thought would change upon marrying her.

The signs of his hardness and temper had been there since the beginning, but she'd allowed infatuation to brush away any concerns. Matthew Mackay had been a distant husband, with a short temper and little patience. Once Finn was born, it was as if he'd no need for a wife and had promptly moved out of their shared bedchamber and never slept with her again.

If she were to guess, he'd never cared for her, but wanted someone, anyone to give him a son.

Her life had become one of constant loneliness. Rambling

about the large house, doing her best to avoid her husband's parents who detested the fact their son had married a woman of such low standing.

Her father was a farmer, her mother a seamstress. They'd provided her and her brother a wonderful, loving home, with plenty of food and clothes. They'd never wanted for anything.

Once married, the only brightness in her days was when she went to visit her parents. She never stayed longer than a day or two, too scared Matthew's family would use her absence as an excuse to throw her out.

Then the horrible day came. Her husband was to travel to the Isle of Barra. It so happened her parents were traveling the same day to visit her brother who lived there. A storm had come upon them suddenly, the turbulent sea too much for the small bìrlinn. Everyone aboard had drowned.

She turned from the window and undressed. Her mind was awhirl with what to do about her mother-in-law. Did the woman seek to have the constable remove Finn from her home? What would happen if she found out about Finn stealing? The first thing she would do the following day would be to approach the constable and find out what they'd discussed.

The Mackays were longtime residents of the Taernsby, but so was she. Her family had been among the first to establish the village. The Mackays had not arrived until after her great-grandparents had been living there for a decade.

She would not allow the woman to take her son. Finn would have to become accustomed to living with her. It had been almost a year since the accident. It was time she became more assertive and stop allowing Finn to spend so much time away from her.

However, the Mackays were of means and had helped the village in ways she could never compete with.

And that was worrisome.

THE SOUNDS OF men's voices woke Robena the next morning with a start. Wrapping a shawl around her, she rushed down the stairs to the front window to peer out. A group of men on horseback rode past at a leisurely pace, scanning the area, as if not wishing to draw notice to themselves.

Could it be they were the attackers whom the man had warned her about? She ducked to the side when one of them turned toward the cottage. There would be little she could do to keep them from entering. Although her front door and back entrance would be hard to penetrate, she wasn't as sure about the shutters.

When she peered out again, they'd gone further, riding to the side of the village where there were fewer houses.

Robena kept watch as the men drew their swords. Then she rushed around the house doing her best to secure every window and both doors.

Once that was completed, she checked on Finn. The boy was fast asleep, so she closed the door to his bedchamber, dressed hurriedly, then went back downstairs to continue her vigil.

CHAPTER FOUR

UPON BEING DISCOVERED, the men who'd been in hiding didn't seem surprised to be confronted by Artair and his men. Instead, with primal yells, they rushed forward at full speed, swords drawn and held over their heads.

"I never understood the need for screaming," Struan said rolling his eyes.

Artair and his men held their steeds back, not willing to draw the fighting too close to the nearest cottages.

When the attackers neared, Artair and Struan rode toward an open area.

Artair did a quick mental assessment of the situation. He had twice as many men—four archers and sixteen warriors. And yet the attackers did not hesitate.

"There are probably more coming," he shouted.

Erik's clear blue eyes narrowed as he scanned the background. "Aye, ye may be right."

The head archer, Ian, called out commands as arrows flew overhead. Two of the invaders fell from their horses, another pair were impaled but still continued forward, clashing with Ross warriors.

Unless more fighters arrived, the battle would be short. Artair rode to one of the fallen men and peered down at him. "Who sent ye?"

The man struggled to breathe, but his gaze held steady on Artair. Seconds later, he went still, his eyes dulled.

The other one was not as injured. He'd struggled to stand and now held the arrow he'd pulled from his body in one hand as he rushed to hide behind a rock.

"Ye can speak or die, yer choice," Artair said pointing his sword at the pale man. "Who sent ye that ye are willing to die for?"

The man spit on the ground, pulled out a dagger and stood. He didn't stand a chance and soon lay dead.

It made little sense. Once again Artair considered that the men knew there was little chance they would win against the Ross' greater numbers.

He rode back to where the others held several of the attackers at sword point. The men knelt with hands on their heads. By the laird's command, prisoners were given a choice of whether to leave the isle forever or die for their cause.

Artair met Struan's gaze, who held a sword directly at a man's throat.

"Where are the rest? I know there are more men," Artair said meeting the man's narrowed gaze. "Tell me or die."

The man spit at Artair. Struan's blade hissed across the man's throat, the prisoner's eyes widened in surprise as dark red spatters sprayed his tunic and the ground below. An instant later, the man toppled to the ground.

"Ye could have allowed me to speak to him more," Artair said giving his friend a pointed look.

Struan shrugged. "He was not going to talk."

It turned out the other six would not speak either. Two were unconscious and the other four remained stoic and silent. With four men dead, Artair considered what to do next.

"Tie them up and we will take them back to the guard post."

He went to where Ian and two other archers kept watch. "Did ye see anyone else?"

The archer looked toward the forest. "No, but they are there. We need more men."

"Darach is sending a large contingency," Artair replied, once again his mind going to why the men were actually there. "It makes little sense. They should be aware these are Ross lands, and we have a huge army."

"They do not understand us," Struan said guiding his horse closer as the prisoners were led away.

"What?" Both Ian and Artair asked at the same time.

"They spoke to each other in a different language," Struan replied. "I am guessing they are Norse perhaps."

"Erik!" Artair called out and the Norseman rode closer. "Do ye speak Norwegian?"

The warrior made a pained expression. "Nay, I never met my grandparents, and my parents did not teach me." He looked toward the prisoners. "Are they Norse?"

Artair shrugged. "I do not know. They do have the coloring. Perhaps come from somewhere else. Struan says they spoke in a different language."

It would make sense that if they were from another land, the attackers were not aware of the size of the Ross army. Also, they did not speak because they did not understand what they'd asked.

Artair looked to Erik. "If my life were on the line, I would make some sort of effort to get my point across."

His friend gave him a bland look. "If they are Norse, they could care less what we want. They hate us."

Along with a group of twenty warriors, Artair and Struan rode away from the village where they suspected the attackers came from.

When they neared the cottage where the woman he'd confronted the day before lived, Artair made a mental note to stop by there on the way back to assure the family they were to be well protected.

"Keep a keen eye out," Artair instructed as they negotiated their way through the thick foliage. There were no clear paths, and it was slow moving. However, it was also obvious people had gone there way recently. Branches had been pushed away and broken, and other plants lay flattened, most likely by horses' hooves.

It was clear the remaining attackers lay in wait when arrows flew at them from a short distance away. An arrow struck Artair, nearly knocking him from his horse, but he managed to put up his shield and hold it up to block more.

Moments later, the clang of metal against metal rang out. Birds in neighboring trees made loud noises of protest as the peacefulness of the forest disappeared, replaced by screams, grunts, and horses neighing.

This time they were almost evenly matched. Artair's archers quickly dispatched several of theirs, however, throughout the fight, arrows continued to rain.

Thankfully, his men were stronger and much better trained in battle and soon the invaders were overtaken. Several fled, while a few surrendered. The archers were the hardest to capture as they silently disappeared into the forest before being caught.

It was hard to tell how many there were in total, but if Artair were to guess, he and his men had been outnumbered.

HE DISMOUNTED AND walked to a tree. Taking a breath, he first broke away the fletched portion of the arrow that protruded. Teeth gritted, he then rammed his shoulder against the tree to push the remaining portion of the arrow out through the other side. He moaned loudly as the tip tore through flesh and muscle, the pain almost sending him to his knees. Panting, he leaned against the tree, waiting for the pain to subside and his vision to clear.

"Ye will need to wrap it tightly," Ian said as he neared. The archer looked around as if expecting bandages to appear out of thin air.

Artair held his right hand over the wound. "I will survive until we reach someone who can help."

He mounted and blew out several breaths to gain his equilibrium, then guided the horse back toward the village. His men would ensure the prisoners were herded to the guard post. Hopefully they would find someone locally who spoke their language and could help question the captured men.

When the familiar cottage came into view, he guided his horse in the direction of the tiny house. Waving the others to continue without him, he dismounted and went to the door.

He pounded the wooden planks several times before the woman finally opened the door. When her gaze moved to the blood soaking though his tunic, her eyes widened. She motioned for him to enter.

"Ye fought," she remarked, going to the fireplace and

pushing a pot over the flames to begin heating.

"Aye," Artair replied. Strange that once again she seemed to be alone. He wondered if the mischievous boy was about.

If the woman was alone, she'd probably ordered the boy to hide while Artair was there. At least that is what he would do if it were his child.

"I only require ye bind my wound so I can be on my way."

She placed a cup in front of him. "For the pain."

Artair drank the liquid greedily. He was thirsty, tired, and in horrible pain. "Thank ye."

Dipping a bowl into the pot, she then brought the hot water and several cloths to the table. "Ye will have to remove yer tunic."

After blowing out several breaths to prepare for the upcoming pain, he grabbed the hem of his tunic and lifted it. Halfway up, he groaned and stopped, arms shaking.

The woman took over and helped him by first removing the right uninjured side and then carefully pulling it over his head and down the left side.

She cringed at seeing the wound. "What did ye do?"

"I pushed the arrow through." Artair looked down. The entire area around the wound was stark purple. A trail of dried blood caked the skin from the wound down to his stomach.

For a moment their eyes met, her dark brown gaze uncertain at meeting his. There was something about her that gave him pause. Unlike the other two times they'd met, this time she seemed vulnerable, almost as if she wanted to say something to him.

"I am Artair Ross." He grunted when she pressed the wet cloth against the wound. "Cousin to the Laird."

She studied him for a moment. "The laird," she whispered, then blew out a breath. "I must speak to him. Can ye arrange for it?"

"I could."

As she cleaned his wound and wrapped a strip of cloths around him, she was silent. Occasionally, she'd glance over her shoulder toward the stairs where Artair guessed the boy was.

"Yer son," Artair began. "Did he make amends for stealing?"

She cringed, almost as if he'd struck her. "Aye, the Millers are having him work for them to repay. I am not certain why he did it."

When her cheeks turned bright pink in embarrassment, Artair felt bad. "I was as mischievous when I was a lad. Tis something young ones do—for fun."

"It is not how he was taught. How he was brought up."

Noting she'd not said, how "she'd" been the one to bring him up, Artair was intrigued. She continued to wrap the bandage around his shoulder, binding his upper left arm tightly against his side, each movement forcing her close. The scent of heather filled the air around them and he guessed she'd washed with soap made from the plant.

"What is yer name?" he asked.

"Robena. My name is Robena Mackay," she stated in a soft voice and once again looked over her shoulder toward the stairs. "Can ye take me to speak to yer cousin? It is very important."

"There are matters I have to see to here. We did not capture all of the encroachers; therefore, my duties remain here for a time."

Her teeth sank into her bottom lip. "Perhaps ye can write a missive. I must speak to the laird."

There wasn't a horse or cart near the cottage. "How will ye travel there?"

At the question, her shoulders fell. "I will ask at the village for someone going to Keep Ross. I am sure someone is."

"Ye do not need a message from me for Darach to see ye. However, I will do it. For now, I must go, there is much to see about."

He struggled into his tunic and walked to the door. "Will ye be in the village tomorrow, Robena?"

She nodded.

"I will find ye."

Immediately her eyes shone with unshed tears, and she took his right hand with both of hers. "Thank ye."

Artair nodded. "It is I who should be thanking ye."

Riding away from the cottage, Artair had a strange feeling. There was something about Robena that pulled to the very core of his being. Yes, there was a strong attraction, the woman was utterly appealing. But it was more than that. It was as if they'd known each other for a long time, or perhaps even been lovers before.

It was a strange sensation that Artair had never experienced before upon meeting someone. Perhaps it was that he'd been alone for too long, or the protective side of him came out at seeing someone so vulnerable.

There had been several moments when he'd felt a strong urge to reach for her, to take her in his arms and reassure her all would be well.

Her situation, whatever it was, was dire. Although she

didn't tell him what occurred, he suspected it had to do with her husband or something of the like. There was no man living at the cottage, he was sure of it. Perhaps she was a widow and wished to request Darach find her a husband or give her sanctuary at the Keep.

Why had he not asked?

By the time he arrived at the post, he was exhausted, and though not as painful as before Robena had bound his wound, his shoulder throbbed.

The building was immense but only had six rooms. A sleeping area, an eating area, three private bedchambers, and kitchen. He walked through the sleeping area and stopped where long tables had been set up for eating.

Men lingered on their cots while some ate, and others were being seen to by the village healer and her helpers.

"There ye are," Erik called out, motioning for him to sit and be served.

Artair grimaced as he settled onto a chair. Alpena, the cook, hurried over, her face flushed. "Young man, ye look as if ye need a proper rest."

"I do Alpena," Artair replied. He held up a bundle of herbs Robena had given him. "Can ye boil these? They will help with the pain."

"Of course, Laddie," the woman replied.

She returned with a tankard of ale and a bowl of meat and vegetables. "Eat now. I will make the tincture for ye."

After eating his fill and drinking the tincture, he could barely keep his eyes open. When Alpena came to pick up the empty bowl, she looked him over. "Go on and rest."

"Do ye know a woman called Robena Mackay?"

"Aye," Alpena replied. "Sad story, that poor lassie. Her husband and parents drowned when their bìrlinn was overturned during a horrible storm."

Artair considered that perhaps Robena was still in mourning. "How long ago?"

"Several seasons ago, perhaps last spring," Alpena replied. "Although the husband was not much of a loss. Horrid man that he was, her parents were wonderful people."

Just then a group of men entered, and Alpena hurried to see about them. "Sit down lads, ye need to eat." The woman was the warm welcome warriors needed upon returning from patrols or battles.

CHAPTER FIVE

After leaving Finn with the Millers, Robena went to work helping an older gardener and his wife with their small crop. There would be plenty of produce to sell the following weeks, which would earn the couple enough coin to last through the fall and winter. They did not require much, as the woman had confided and therefore what they earned from the produce as more than enough.

The older woman spun wool to make their clothes and bedding. The couple bartered for many things, and their small herd of goats and chickens provided milk, meat and eggs.

Robena worked for them in exchange for food which they gave her whenever she came to help. It was a learning experience so she would be able to support Finn and provide for herself.

At the moment, she did not trust men enough to wish to marry again and needed to ensure she was able to support her son by working.

Despite living a short distance from the village, it would be possible to sell something to earn coin. She'd considered baskets, pottery, or such and discarded each idea. Finally, she settled on selling produce like the older couple did. There were many fishermen and wives who came to the square every day to purchase food. One more vendor would be welcome.

When Robena finished weeding and transplanting young seedlings, she gathered her shawl and basket which had oat flour and eggs to make bread. It would go perfectly with the leftover fish stew from the day before.

The village square was busy as the last of the sales were made and people were in a hurry to go home and prepare their evening meals.

"Robena, how are ye?" a woman asked as she walked by. Her name was Heather, a jovial woman, just a year older than Robena, who seemed to be constantly with child. Two young bairns hung by her skirts and she carried another on her hip. A basket filled with her purchases hung from her elbow.

She and Heather had been friends since childhood.

Robena kissed each child, hugging Heather last. "What are ye making for supper?"

"Roasted lamb with herbs, and leak and potato pie." Heather smacked her lips. "Ye should join us."

"I suppose we can," Robena replied, excited at the chance to not have to cook. "Let me gather Finn and we'll come around."

Heather gave her a puzzled look. "I just passed him and that horrid woman Elena Mackay. Saw him climb in her carriage and head out of the village."

The ground swayed and Robena closed her eyes as helplessness enveloped. Of course, the woman had taken advantage that Finn was alone. The boy loved his grandmother and would have no qualms going with her.

Afraid of falling, Robena held her arms out, it was of no avail, she slumped to the ground.

"Oh dear." Heather did her best to reach out, but with the

bairns and basket, she gave up and instead looked at her friend with sorrow-filled eyes. "I am so sorry. I thought ye knew."

After a moment, Robena staggered to her feet. Then she lifted her basket and shoved it at the already overwhelmed Heather.

"Please keep this for me. I must go and fetch him."

ROBENA RAN AS fast as her skirts allowed in the direction of the Mackay's house. It was on the opposite side of the village, up a hill and then down a long road. By the time she reached the hill, her lungs burned from the exertion and still she had a long way to go.

Her tears had dried and were replaced by outrage. How dare the woman take Finn without permission?

The thunder of hooves made her hesitate and she whirled to find a group of horsemen upon her. Robena raced toward the safety of trees, but she was not fast enough.

Someone reached down and grabbed her by the waist of her skirts and flung her over his horse. Robena screamed, kicking and fighting in an effort to get away.

Losing her balance, she slipped and hung down the side of the horse, her skirt flowing over her head, not allowing her to see much other than the passing ground beneath.

Whoever the horseman was, grunted and yanked her back up, then he roughly pulled her up against his chest. "*Vær stille.*"

They were not familiar, and she turned to see the others. A bearded man came alongside. He eyed her with disdain and said something to her captor in a language she did not understand.

Her captor replied in a harsh tone and shook his head. It appeared to her that the other man did not want her along.

The horses were galloping now. Robena had no idea in which direction they headed. She'd become disoriented and upon catching her breath, struggled wildly as she did her best to figure it out. Her captor held the reins with the hand around her waist and used his left hand to smack her in the face.

She was momentarily blinded by the pain, the coppery taste of blood in her mouth.

They rode through the woods, so she could not see the shore. Overhead, the thick branches came together, forming a canopy through which she could barely see the sky. She turned to look behind—there were only a pair of additional men. Whether one or four, it mattered little as she doubted to be able to fight them off.

"Let me go!" she screamed elbowing her captor in the ribs. "Let me go!"

"*Hold kjeft*," He growled in her ear, his arms tightening around her in an unmovable vice. Her breathing soon became ragged.

"Ye're hurting me." She gasped, attempting to breathe.

Thankfully, he loosened his grip a bit, but not enough that it gave any room for her to hit him. Arms pinned to her sides, Robena was trapped for the moment.

Finn was safe. The thought crossed her mind and she let out a long sigh. Despite being with that hateful woman, he would be kept safe as the Mackays had guardsmen and could provide the safety she never could.

Her beautiful boy. An errant tear rolled down her cheek at the realization these men would use her at will and probably kill her. There was no mercy in their expressions. They had been nearby for only a few weeks, each time they appeared only to attack and kill. They'd burned several homes to the ground, had killed men who'd tried to defend their families.

All for what? It made little sense.

Now, in all probability she would be another of their victims. There was little doubt in her mind what would happen upon reaching their campsite. And her son would be raised by the Mackays. Would he grow up to be like his father?

"Please let me go!" she screamed again only for her captor to momentarily release his grip on her waist and gripped her forearm with so much force she whimpered.

He repeated the same words as before and Robena deduced it meant for her to be quiet. Perhaps in a less kind way.

Her arm throbbed and she slumped forward and cried.

A long while later, they entered a small clearing nestled against the slope of a hill.

Everyone dismounted. The man who'd she ridden with yanked her forward, his grip tight on her arms, making her wince. When she fought against him, a hard slap sent her reeling sideways until she fell to the ground. The side of her face burned, and the split lip bled anew.

There were others there, but most did not seem to find what happened between her and her captor interesting, other than a glance to her every once in a while.

The man pushed her to the ground and tied her wrists together. He then half dragged her to a tree and tied her to it. Finally, he tore a strip from her skirts and wrapped it around the lower half of her face.

It was hard to breathe. The idiot had covered her mouth and nose. Robena took ragged breaths, attempting to suck air through the fabric. It didn't help that terror gripped her and she could not stop crying.

A man said something, pointing at her while chuckling. She gathered he pointed out that with both her nose and mouth covered, she could not breathe.

The same man who'd tied her up, stomped over and yanked the gag beneath her nose. Robena inhaled deeply, her mind whirling as to how to get away. She adjusted herself to determine how tight the rope was that bound her to the tree. It loosened just a bit and she realized the knot was slipping and would not hold long. All she had to do was find the right moment to pull and hopefully it would untie.

Meanwhile, the men had gathered in a circle. The four who'd ridden from the village spoke to another pair who'd been waiting there.

Now there were six. It would be harder to slip away since several faced her. Whatever the men were discussing, however, seemed to take all the attention. She kept her eyes on them as she gently pulled on the rope. The knot gave way, and the rope went slack, landing across her tied wrists. Robena kept still so it was not too obvious it was loose.

One of the men yelled at another who responded with a punch to the face. Several grabbed the two to separate them.

Robena shimmied to the side of the tree, then with all that remained of her strength, she jumped to her feet and ran into the thick brush. Branches cut her arms and face, but she barely felt it as she pushed through, running as fast as she could.

The men's voices sounded farther and farther away as they continued arguing. Hopefully, they'd not notice she'd escaped until she could find a place to safely hide. She was smart enough to know that she could not outrun men on horses, but she could find a place to hide until they gave up.

It was becoming harder to keep going, her body protesting against her running for so long. Between the throbbing arm and the cuts and scratches, her mouth was dry and yet she knew it could mean death if she stopped moving.

Just as she was about to give up, she saw a small bush with bright red berries. To the side of it another one and between them a hollow where she could crawl.

Robena studied her surroundings. To her right was a passable area, she went to it and pushed branches back for a few yards and then backtracked. Hopefully, whoever followed would think she went in that direction.

Finally, she crawled between the berry bushes, doing her best not to disturb the branches. Once ensconced there, she reached out through the branches and carefully replaced twigs and leaves near the opening.

She sat back, pulling her knees up against her chest and laid her head atop and inhaled deeply until her she was no longer out of breath. In the quiet, she waited, listening intently for the sounds of men approaching. All she heard was birdsong and chirping of insects of some sort. It seemed the wildlife had accepted her presence.

It was much later—at least it seemed to her it was as she'd fallen asleep—that her heart quickened at hearing men's voices in the distance.

From where she was, Robena could not tell if it was her

captors or others. It was safer to remain put until hopefully the next day she could think clearer and decipher where exactly she was.

When darkness fell, so did Robena's spirits. She'd not heard voices or horses again, but she'd been too terrified to move from where she was. In the darkness she wouldn't be able to move as easily, but hopefully she could head in the right direction.

After crawling from her hiding place, Robena looked up past the trees to the sky. The full moon shined bright, illuminating the forest, giving it a magical feel.

With tentative steps, she walked in the direction of the path she'd seen earlier and then continued, praying for something to show her in which direction to go.

Moments later, the sound of the waves lapping on the shore brought tears to her eyes. She was up the coast somewhere. Unfortunately, to go to the shore would mean being out in the open, so she remained in the woods, walking in the direction she hoped to find the village.

Her stomach growled, demanding food and drink. There wouldn't be any for a while yet. Not until she found someone to help her.

It seemed to take forever to make progress. Every so often she stopped to get her bearings, still unsure if she traveled in the right direction. It was much later that she saw the familiar portion of land which jutted out where fishermen's shacks and boats lined the shore. She was still a distance from the village, but when she reached the fishing village, she would be safe.

Deciding it was best to wait until morning, once again she found a place to hide and settled under foliage to rest.

This time she woke to the thundering of many horses racing past in the direction she'd come.

It was the Ross army. She was sure of it.

Robena raced out from the woods, waving her arms to get someone's attention. A warrior slowed and glowered down at her. "What is it?"

"Is Artair Ross with ye? I was taken by the attackers. I know where they hide."

His expression relaxed. "Yer Robena Mackay then?"

When she nodded, he called out.

"Here is the woman we are in search of!"

CHAPTER SIX

ARTAIR SWUNG HIS war horse around and galloped back to where Robena stood, looking up at one of the warriors. Her clothes were dirty, the hem of her skirts torn, and her hair flew about in a tangle of curls.

When he dismounted and went to her, she broke down. Through her sobs, she attempted to tell him what had occurred.

With so many looking on, all he could do was awkwardly pat her back. "How did ye get away?"

When she looked up, his chest clenched at seeing the bruising. The left side of her face was swollen and purpling. Her lip was split, dried blood still on it.

"Who hit ye?"

"The man who took me. They are camped beside the hills, near a small cave. I walked from there, so it is in that direction." She pointed past him through the woods.

"Ye will have to come with me. I cannot leave ye here alone."

Robena nodded. By her rounded shoulders and the way she slumped against him, it was obvious she was exhausted. However, they needed her in order to find the hideaway.

When he touched her upper arm, she winced and gasped in pain.

"Help me get her onto my horse," he instructed the warrior who'd come upon her. His injury remained painful, and he did not wish to make it worse.

Once he mounted, the man lifted Robena up to his arms. She didn't protest, instead let out a breath and remained silent.

The warrior rode off to tell the leaders in which direction to go and the army of over two hundred warriors continued forth.

He pulled out his wineskin and handed it to Robena, who drank from it greedily. "Thank ye."

"I do not have any food." Artair suspected that she'd not drank or eaten since being taken the afternoon before.

It had been a pair of hours after she'd been abducted before a man had arrived to inform them of having seen Robena taken away.

Since the men who'd taken her were not familiar to the villager, it was obvious that it was the attackers who'd stolen her. Unfortunately, they'd had to wait until almost daybreak to leave, since the army from the keep was yet to arrive.

Despite having traveled since before dawn, the warriors did not seem weary. After training for months and living in relative peace, the men were ready to fight to defend the lands.

"How did ye get away?" Artair asked her as they continued forth. What he really wanted to know was what the men had done to her. Obviously, there was only one reason to steal a woman.

"They were fighting, and I took the opportunity to escape," she replied in a tight voice. "The one who hit me is very violent."

"How many were there?"

"I only saw six. There were four who took me and two more at the campsite. I do not know if that was all of them."

He considered asking more, but decided she'd been through enough without him making her relive whatever happened during the hours she was with the men.

"How many?" It was Erik who'd approached to ask. Artair related the information Robena had told him. The Norseman's gaze flickered to Robena, narrowing upon noting the bruising.

"We'll kill the bastard," he informed Robena, who tensed.

When Erik rode away, she turned to look up at him. "Why must it all be about violence and hate? My mother-in-law hates me. I do not know why. She took Finn." She hesitated for a moment as a sob escaped. "I am so very tired of it all."

"Did the boy go willingly?"

"Aye, he prefers to live there than with me. His entire life, they kept us apart. I only saw him occasionally. I do not blame Finn for it."

It was not the time for him to give an opinion. However, Artair wondered if perhaps it was best for the young lad to be raised by his father's family.

When they arrived near the area where Robena recalled the enemy camp, Artair looked to his men who held their steeds back waiting for the trackers to deduce in which direction the encroachers had gone.

Most of the warriors formed a large barrier, surrounding the area. Although those nearby could possibly escape away from the road, the foliage was much too dense to do so on horseback.

It was only moments later that the attackers emerged from the woods. About twenty men on horseback, swords raised.

Upon seeing the size of the army that awaited them, they lost their bravado after only a few moments of clashes with the warriors who'd discovered them.

The fight was anti-climactic. The men quickly surrendered, or, in the case of the one which Robena pointed out to be her attacker, quickly dispatched.

His cousin Duncan, a huge warrior, rode up to them. "Darach wishes to see ye," he said. "Ye should go with us to the keep from here."

Artair looked to Robena. "Aye, I can. We will pass by her cottage. I can leave her there on the way."

"Nay," Robena said in a strong voice. "I am coming with ye. I must speak to the laird."

ARTAIR INSTRUCTED THE warriors to bring the prisoners to the southern post, where they'd get carts to take the captured men back to Clan Ross keep for questioning. Whoever was behind the attacks had to be someone who wanted something specific. So far, the attacks had been random and perhaps it was just that, men with no other reason than to kill and pillage.

Besides, the only person Artair knew of who had enough coin to hire so many men, or cause harm to the clan was their enemy, Cairn McInerny. His cousin Caelan had killed Cairn, so he was no longer a threat.

If these warriors been hired by him, it was possible the invaders were not aware of Cairn's demise. Either way, it was best to take them somewhere and get the truth out of them. There were men at the keep who spoke other languages and would find out more.

As they rode back at a more leisurely pace, Artair wondered what to do about Robena. They did not have any carts other than those that would be used to transport prisoners. The others were used by Alpena for trips to the market.

It was a long ride back to the keep—a day at least. She would have to ride with him on Hagar.

"I will take ye to yer home to collect things. We depart for the keep at dawn."

ARTAIR PACED IMPATIENTLY as Robena hurried about collecting items. He'd insisted she take her time.

He'd drawn water for her from the well and waited outside while she washed and donned fresh clothes. When he'd entered again, she looked like the woman he recalled upon first meeting her. The swelling on her face had gone down some, only the purpling remaining from the strike.

Other than a piece of bread, he'd not noticed her eating anything else. Artair made a mental note to ask Alpena to prepare something for Robena when they arrived at the guard post.

Finally, she walked down the stairs, her expression drawn. "I do not know why, but it feels as if I will not return here again."

"Ye will…if ye wish," Artair reassured her. "There is no reason for ye to feel that way."

She walked closer carrying a large bag that he took from her. Upon nearing, their gazes met, and he noted when he leaned forward just a bit to study the bruising, her eyes widened and she took a deep breath.

Aye, there was definitely something strong between them.

"Artair," she said, her voice almost a whisper.

He looked into her eyes. "Aye?"

"Tell me all will be well and I will have my son again. That I will be happy one day."

His heart broke for her, the poor woman had gone through so much and she clung to the tiniest bit of hope to survive.

He could say the words, but it would be only that, words. A long time ago, he'd made a vow never to promise something he did not believe was possible. However, this was different, with her, the protector in him needed to ensure she would be well and happy.

Setting the bag on the floor, he took Robena by the shoulders.

"Look at me." She did and for a long moment, he held her gaze, doing his best to give her reassurance."

"All will be well . . ." Instead of finishing the rest of the sentence, he pulled her close and held her as she clung to him and cried. Her entire body shook with each sob, the pain so piercing he felt it go through him.

"Cry now Robena, but ye must be strong. Brave for yerself and yer lad."

"I-I do not think I can," she sputtered between sobs. "I cannot possibly."

Letting out a breath, he knew it was best to be firm. As much as he wished to give her time to grieve, there wasn't time and the sooner they left, the better. Otherwise, he would drag her up the stairs and make love to her until they both forgot all that had happened.

"We must go," he whispered, not wishing for her to pull away, but there was much to do, and he could not afford to linger.

When she lifted her face, he pressed a soft kiss to her lips. To his astonishment, the simple touch between them sent tingles down his spine. What was he, a lad giving his first kiss?

Robena's lips curved just a bit. "Thank ye for everything. Ye are so very kind."

Had the kiss not affected her like him? Artair cleared his throat and bent to pick up the bag. Enough foolishness. He needed to act like a grown man and do what was needed.

"How does your injury fare? You seem recovered. It is so soon," Robena meeting his gaze.

Artair did not want to burden her with the fact it hurt quite a bit. He'd not fought that day on purpose knowing he'd in all probability be killed.

"My injury is not a concern."

"It must still hurt ye," she insisted.

"Aye, it does."

ONCE THEY ARRIVED at the guard post, Robena would have to tell them everything that had happened and what she heard while abducted. He hated to make her relive it, but it could prove to be lifesaving for the villagers.

"Come we must go." He lifted the bag then helped her bar the door from the outside. Without meaning to, he placed his hand on the small of her back when they walked to the horse.

Catching himself, he could not figure out what to do. Remove it? No, she'd think him affected. Leave it? Would she find him too familiar? In the end, he coughed and moved his hand over his mouth.

Once they neared the steed, he motioned to the horse. "Can ye mount?"

She nodded and with only a bit of assistance manage to hoist herself into the saddle. Then he secured her bag to the saddle and mounted behind her. Her bottom was much too close and settled between his legs. That was definitely dangerous. How the bloody hell was he to make it for an entire day with her so close?

When he adjusted backward in the saddle, Robena shifted and settled so that she was flush against him again. Not seeming to notice or care that he took a fortifying breath, she relaxed.

"Do ye know how to gut a deer?" he asked.

She shook her head. "I do not think so."

As they rode, Artair explained how to remove the pelt, where to cut it and what to keep and throw away. Picturing what he spoke about kept his mind occupied so the movement of the horse and the sway of her bottom against him did not have too much of an effect.

It was obvious by her lack of response that she was not at all interested in what he spoke of. Probably thought him a bit eccentric that he picked the topic at a time when neither of them would be killing a deer.

However, the distraction worked for them both. His arousal lessened and for a few moments she could not think about her situation.

UPON ARRIVING AT the post, Alpena took over and settled Robena at a table in the kitchen with a huge bowl of food in front of her. "Ye need yer strength lass. If ye are to go to Keep Ross, it is a long trip."

Artair went in search of Erik and Struan. He found them

with the prisoners, who had been fed bread and given water, and were now loaded into cages on the back of three carts.

"We will head out immediately," Struan explained, pushing back the dark hair blowing across his face with impatience. "We do not have the space to keep them here."

"That is a good idea," Artair replied, eyeing the men who glared from the confines of the cages.

The sooner they were able to find out why they were here, the better.

Artair went back inside to find Robena and walked with her to the bedchamber he'd been using.

Bryce sat up from one of the cots in there. "Ye plan to sleep in here with her?" He gave him a surprised look.

"No," Artair said with a shake of his head. "Ye and I will be sleeping out in the main room."

"There are no bunks left," Bryce said and flopped backward onto the bed, crossed his arms over his chest and closed his eyes.

"I can sleep in the kitchen," Robena offered looking at Bryce with curiosity. "I do not wish to be a bother."

Artair glared at Bryce, who now pretended to sleep. Or perhaps he did.

"No ye can stay. I will find a place to sleep." He studied Bryce. "If my brother comes near ye, ye have my permission to stab him."

At that Bryce opened his eyes, looked at Robena and then narrowed his eyes at Artair. "Ye are an idiot."

In the end, Bryce was right. With all the guards that had arrived, there wasn't an inch on the floor in the main room to spare. Artair ended up sleeping on the floor in the room with Robena and Bryce.

CHAPTER SEVEN

IT HAD BEEN an exhausting day. Despite sharing a room with the brothers, Robena had slept deeply. She'd woken early to the sounds of snores and slipped from the room to find Alpena.

"Did ye rest?" Alpena said, seeming not to find it at all odd that she'd slept in a room with men she barely knew.

Her cheeks burned hot. "Surprisingly well despite . . . the situation."

"Ah," Alpena replied. "Mister Artair is a man of honor; I am sure he did not try anything untoward. And he keeps the young one in check."

Robena looked around at the other cooks and moved closer so she could whisper to Alpena. "It is still most unsettling."

"It is an unsettling time, dear. Our village is under attack. Ye were taken by force. No one will think anything of it." Alpena shrugged and whispered. "Besides other than myself, I do not think anyone knows. Mister Artair assured me ye were safe and said he would leave the door cracked a bit in case I felt the need to check on ye."

"Good." Robena felt better and with that, she went to the side door and washed her face and hands with water from a collection barrel. After doing her best finger-combing and braiding her hair, she went back into the kitchen to help cook.

They'd barely begun feeding the guards when Artair appeared and insisted she eat her fill so they could leave.

As she ate, he sat at the table and removed his tunic. A woman, who she assumed was the healer, came over and unwrapped the bandages around his shoulder and cleaned the wound.

Robena did her best not to gawk. His body was perfectly formed, a dusting of hair from his chest down to the edge of his breeches.

When he looked to her and caught her looking, her breath hitched. "Yer wound seems to be healing well."

He nodded. "Aye, it is no longer as painful as it was."

THE RIDE TO Keep Ross was exhausting. Despite riding with Artair, who seemed tireless, Robena had to fight the urge to lean back against him and sleep. It would be much too familiar, but at the same time, she wasn't sure how long it would be before she could not stop from dozing off.

The rocking motion of the horse, plus the fact the guards didn't seem to feel a need to stop, made it worse.

"Are ye not in pain from all the jostling?" Robena asked.

Artair grunted. "I am, but not as bad as other injuries. I have been in many battles. Ye could say I am used to it."

She couldn't imagine it.

It seemed only a moment later she woke with a start. She'd slumped sideways against his shoulder and fallen asleep.

Robena quickly straightened. "I am so sorry. Yer arm must be numb."

"Yer head was on my healthy shoulder. It did not bother me," he replied sounding as if in a good mood.

"Are we almost there?" Robena wiped her face with the back of her hand then looked around at the unfamiliar territory.

"Aye the Keep is just ahead up there on the right."

Her eyes widened at taking in the structure that blended with the background of steep, craggy, misty mountains. The high walls surrounding the structure were made of gray stones and the arched gates were iron masterpieces clutching thick wooden planks. She leaned forward.

"It is beautiful."

"Aye it is." There was pride in his voice. "*Duin Láidir*, is my family's legacy. The castle was built by our great-grandfather."

It made sense for it to be called Silver Castle. The color of the huge home seemed to shimmer in the sun.

"Tell me about the laird," Robena said, suddenly nervous about meeting the man who was called The Lion. He sounded intimidating.

"Darach is stern but fair. He has a hound called Albie which he adores. They go for long walks daily. Sometimes we think the hound is his advisor."

Despite the nerves, Robena chuckled. "I love dogs."

"Do ye live here?" She asked, wanting to know more about the man she'd spent so many hours with as of late.

"I have no true home. I live here and at my parent's home which is closer to Taernsby."

Robena considered he didn't sound bothered by the fact he had no place to call a true home. "Do ye not wish for a place of yer own?"

She felt his shoulders lift and lower. "No. I am content to go where I am needed. I have no need for a house or anything of the like. Attachment to things makes one weak."

The statement shook her. The most important thing she felt an attachment to was Finn. And now he'd been torn from her.

"Perhaps ye are correct. However, a child is different," Robena stated. "Ye cannot help but feel as if they are a part of ye and will do anything for them. Finn is my only attachment in life. It does not make me weaker, but stronger. I will do what it takes for my son."

"Does that include giving him up to someone who can offer him a better life?"

At the question, she wanted to swing around and glared at him. Fury coursed through her. "I am his mother. A child should be with who loves them the most."

"We arrive," Artair replied without emotion.

Robena closed her eyes to keep the angry tears from slipping. How could a man who had no wish for a home or stability begin to understand what it was like to lose one's child?

In that moment she wanted to be away from him, to rush into the keep and demand to speak to the laird immediately.

The sooner she was back in her cottage with her son, the better.

UPON DEPOSITING HER at the kitchen entrance, Artair had disappeared without a word. Perhaps he sensed she was angry and wisely made himself scarce.

"Welcome to Keep Ross." A young servant who introduced herself as Finella greeted her, motioning to a doorway.

Finella was the kind of pretty that came from contentment. With a fair face, freckles across the bridge of her nose, and hair neatly pinned under a cap, Robena instantly liked her.

"Come in and rest." Finella ushered Robena to a small dining room beside the kitchen. It was obviously where the servants ate and rested.

"I came to speak to the laird. It is very important," Robena said, her voice already trembling.

Finella gave her a knowing look and patted her hand. "The Laird is gone to a family gathering. His brother Ewan, who lives north of here, is hosting it. He and Lady Isobel will not return until sometime tomorrow."

"Tomorrow," Robena repeated, her stomach sinking. "I suppose there is little that can be done until then. What can I do to help?"

The woman's face brightened. "Ye just came from a long ride. I will show ye a room where ye can rest and then after ye have a wee sleep, ye can help with last meal if ye wish."

After sharing a light meal with Finella and her mother Gara, who was the keep housekeeper and cook, Robena was ushered to a small but tidy room to rest.

Despite her anxiousness, she quickly fell into a deep slumber, waking confused a few hours later.

Upon emerging from the corridor where she'd slept, she stopped and gawked. The great room was filled with people. Some looked to be of high station, others humbler. And yet everyone seemed to have a place at long tables with large candelabras in the centers. Servants passed by with huge trays of steaming food and swiftly worked from table to table placing the offerings before those seated.

At the high board were three men, one of them Artair. To his side was a large muscular male who spoke with him. By their similar coloring and features, she expected they were related. The man turned to take in the room. His gaze moved across the expanse, meeting hers for a long moment.

Extremely handsome and with a commanding air, he had to be a Ross. The man said something to Artair, who looked toward her and stood.

Unsure what to do, she remained still until he neared.

"Do ye wish to sit with us for last meal as my guest?"

He was leaving the option open, though she felt totally inadequate, not only because of her dress, which was crumpled from the travel, but also because she was nothing more than a villager. However, for Finn's sake, she would do anything.

Robena nodded. "Aye, thank ye."

Upon reaching the high board, the large muscular man stood and held out a chair. "Please sit." His voice was deep and something about the way he kept his distance made her extra careful not to go too near.

"This is my cousin, Duncan Ross, second born to the laird," Artair explained. "He is here in Darach's stead."

Sitting between the two, Robena felt tongue-tied and anxious. "I am Robena Mackay," she said to Duncan who slid a glance to her and nodded in response.

"Did ye not wish to join in the family celebration?" Robena asked.

He let out a breath, not as if exasperated, but more as if he wasn't sure what to say. "Someone has to remain behind to take my brother's place."

It made sense.

Artair had placed meat and vegetables on her plate and was lathering butter on bread when she looked to him. He set it next to the other food. "Eat."

Daring to look around the room, she scanned it quickly. Most of the people at the tables ate and spoke to others near them, while the guards mostly ate in silence. At one particularly close table, there was a family, who by their dress were of high station. Perhaps visitors.

It was then she turned her attention to the man who sat beside Artair. He was older, perhaps ten years more than him. The man was discussing their travels and hopes to have time to speak about matters with Darach before leaving.

Artair was assuring him the laird would return the next day.

Sensing someone looking at her, Robena returned her attention back to the high station table. There was a woman about her age who glared in her direction. The woman was attractive with an intricate hairstyle and low-cut bodice. Their gazes met and the woman narrowed her eyes and pressed her lips into a tight line.

Robena quickly looked down at her food.

"What do ye seek to speak to my brother about?" Duncan asked.

Her chest immediately tightened. "My son has been taken by my late husband's family, the Mackays. I wish for the laird to order he be returned to me." Her voice shook and she took a drink from her cup. "He is all I have."

The laird's brother nodded. "I do not think to know the

Mackays," he replied. "Are they mistreating yer son?"

"No," Robena shook her head, not willing to lie. "Quite the opposite, they dote on him. However, they will raise him to be like his father, austere and uncaring about others."

He did not reply right away, instead his hazel gaze met hers for a moment. There was understanding and something heartbreaking about him so that she felt an urge to weep. Not wanting to make a fool of herself, Robena tore bread and dipped it into the meat juices. Taking several bites, she realized the food was the best she'd ever eaten.

"Missus Mackay," Duncan said taking her attention again. "Who a man grows to become can be influenced by his upbringing, but he will be his own person. Do not discount yer part in his life."

Artair touched her arm. "Eat."

Despite twice the men seeming to think Finn was not in a bad place, which left her hollow, Robena ate.

"The cook here creates magic," she said to Artair who nodded.

"Which is why our great room is always filled. Somedays, we close the gates to keep them away, because the family needs to rest from it."

"How long before I can return and see about Finn, do ye think?" Robena was anxious to get a missive from the laird and return to her village.

Artair shook his head. "There are tasks I must see to. It could be several days. I would not plan on returning for at least a sennight."

Her heart sank. So long? Would the laird take that long to see her? Or perhaps he would find out more before granting her exclusive rights to her son?

She pushed from the table. "If ye will excuse me. I wish to help Gara." No one tried to stop her as she hurried through the room toward the kitchen. Walking past it to find a garden, she opened the gate and walked in past the plants, shed, and tools until finding a bench. Robena sank onto it and gave in to grief.

Sobs racked through her, the heartbreak of not knowing how long before she could see Finn. Without even a cart or horse, it wasn't as if she could travel to at least try to visit. She'd had to sell those items to survive after her husband's family had asked her to leave their home.

If the laird did not agree Finn should live with her, she would have little option but to find and abduct her son and then flee as far as possible.

To hire a bìrlinn and start over would take coin, which she had very little of. Overwhelmed by all that hit at once, she continued to cry.

At the sound of footsteps, Robena wiped her eyes and nose and sniffed loudly, doing her best to compose herself. However, it was impossible. Her broken heart barely allowed her to breathe.

"Robena." Artair walked closer and looked down at her. "What happened?"

How to explain the despondence she felt? "I am worried about Finn and whether or not I will ever have him again. I miss him."

He took her shoulders and pulled her to stand. "I will do all I can to help ye so yer boy will be returned to ye."

"What if it is not what is best for him? What if I am mistaken to pull him from the life he's always known? Am I being selfish?"

Artair was quiet. Of course, he had no idea what the right answer was. She didn't either. The one thing she did know was that she wanted to be part of Finn's life. Nothing would keep her from letting Finn know how much she loved him.

"Come." He took her elbow and guided her out of the garden. They walked out the front gates and up a slight hill that overlooked the inlet in front of the keep. It was almost sunset, and the guards appeared as shadows as they patrolled atop the thick walls.

To the left was the direction where she lived and Robena looked to the trees, in her mind visualizing the village and the hill upon which the Mackays lived. One would have to travel a road along the woods' edge where she'd been taken.

An involuntary shudder went through her.

"Here. Sit." They lowered to sit on a thick tartan Artair had placed on the ground. In silence, she watched the ebb and flow of the waves and little birds racing along the water's edge, pecking at the sand.

It was a beautiful view and with the slight breeze fanning across her face and a protective man on her side, it would be one of the most perfect moments of her life. If not for the fact that Robena needed to be close to Finn, she'd never want to leave.

"Do ye think yer great-grandfather stood here and, taken by its beauty, decided to build?" Robena asked as several wagons rolled out through the gates. Families returning home after a good meal.

"I would not doubt it," Artair replied.

When she shivered, he placed an arm around her shoulders and pulled her against his side. The gesture was unexpected, and yet it felt natural. They'd spent so much time lately in close proximity, it was as if they fell into a sort of kinship.

However, she could not allow emotions free reign with Artair. He'd already made it clear that settling was not something he wanted.

What she craved the most was stability. She'd wished for nothing more all her life than the security of a loving husband, a family, and a home.

Robena turned to tell Artair her wishes for the future. Their close proximity took her breath. When his mouth pressed against hers, she gave in to the kiss, her eyes closing as her body came to life with sensations she'd never felt before.

Clinging to his broad shoulders, she returned the kiss, needing to feel alive and wanted. Never in her life had she felt so close to someone, and yet how could it be? She didn't know him well at all.

When his arms circled around and Artair pulled her against him, she melted. For those few moments in his arms as every part of her came to life, she wished it would never end.

It was dangerous. He was not the kind of man who would ever commit and yet for some reason it was as if his presence was enough.

Robena pushed back, breaking the kiss. They stared at each other, chests heaving and, at least for her, her heart thundering. Still his arms remained around her, but a bit loser.

"I did not mean to overstep," Artair said, releasing her. At once she felt chilled and she pulled her shawl tighter around her shoulders.

"Ye did not," Robena assured him. "It is not as if I did not enjoy the attention, or the distraction," she added with a soft smile.

His gaze searched hers. "It is not the right time. I understand."

She should never give in or lay with him. As attracted as she was to Artair Ross, he was a man with no home and no want of a family.

Instead, she sighed. "It is best we do not kiss again. I cannot afford to lose my mind right now." Robena searched his face. "One day, I plan to settle with a husband, and I can only hope his kisses are as wonderful."

Artair laughed. "I appreciate the compliment."

He held out a hand. "I will escort ye inside. I have to meet with the others and find out what they've discovered after speaking to the men we captured."

"I do not want to see them," Robena said. "Please."

"Ye will not have to. Although my cousin may wish to ask ye about the experience upon his return tomorrow."

They went inside and as they entered the great room, the young woman who'd glared at Robena earlier appeared.

"Ah there ye are, Artair. I have been searching for ye everywhere." She glanced to Robena, her calculating gaze traveling up her body before returning to Artair. "Would ye join us in the parlor for some brandy? As ye know, my father imports only the best."

"Aye thank ye, Clara, I will be there shortly," Artair replied. When the woman didn't move, he looked to Robena. "Would ye like to join us?"

Clara's eyebrows lifted and she gave them an astounded look. "I am sure this woman would never understand the intricacies of my father's brandy."

"Artair," Duncan stood at a doorway. "A word."

As he walked away, Robena remained standing before the woman. She had so many rebuttals to what the horrid woman had said but decided to bite her tongue. Obviously, the woman was a friend of the Ross' and there was no need to make an enemy of someone who could affect the reply to her plea.

"Ye should not set yer sights so high," the woman said, her dark eyes glued to Robena's. "I am sure there are plenty of guardsmen who can give ye what ye seek."

"Good night," Robena said and hurried away, not quite sure where to go.

CHAPTER EIGHT

AFTER HELPING TO set up the dining hall for the morning meal the next day, Robena sat by one of the hearths. Restless, she'd been keeping an eye out for the laird, who'd returned but had yet to make an appearance.

This was something she had to do on her own and did not require Artair to intercede. There was little he could do more than introduce her, and from what she'd witnessed with his brother Duncan, people who came to speak to the laird waited for their turn and then approached with whatever their requests or grievances were.

Murmurs rose and she looked up.

When the laird appeared in the room, there was no mistaking who he was. Tall and well built, with a beautiful golden mane, he made his way down the stairs and through the room.

He didn't seem to notice how much attention he demanded and instead made his way to guards whom he spoke to briefly, even laughing loudly at something one said.

Immediately, Robena got to her feet and hurried closer to the high board. It was early yet, and many had not arrived. It seemed those who lingered were those who lived in the keep.

A couple came to stand near where Robena was, seeming to need to laird's attention as well.

Darach Ross was as everyone had described him, ruggedly

handsome with a stern expression, but at the same time approachable. He was not intimidating as she'd expected. Still, her hands trembled, and she clutched them at her waist, waiting for him to notice her.

To her dismay, he motioned for the couple to come forward and they began a long discussion about whatever they were there for. From what she could overhear, it had something to do with a relative's death and the survivors throwing them off their land.

Refusing to move, as she expected to be next, she remained rooted to the spot.

A guard was called over and the laird gave orders that they accompany the couple to their home and do something or other. Robena couldn't hear over the thundering echoes of her heart beats.

"Are ye waiting to speak to me?"

The laird's words brought her senses to a more reasonable level, and she nodded, moving closer. "I am, Laird. I come to speak to ye about my son. He has been taken."

His hazel gaze reminded her of Artair. The laird studied her for a long moment. "I do not believe we have met before. What is yer name?"

How silly of her not to have led with an introduction.

"I apologize," Robena said feeling small. "I am Robena Mackay." She lowered to a curtsy.

His expression didn't change, other than to look toward the kitchen. Robena wondered if perhaps he'd not eaten yet.

"Laird," she said, getting his attention. "My deceased husband's family took my son, Finn. He belongs with me. I am his mother and should be the one to raise him." At this point, she couldn't help the tears that flowed down her face.

"Laird, I beg of ye, help me get my son back. He is all I have."

The laird lowered his gaze for a long moment, seeming to consider her request. She could only stand before him, wringing her hands.

"The Mackays were here to see me a few days ago. To request the same. I was informed by them that ye have no proper way to provide for the boy."

Her heart sank. Of course, the horrible woman would ensure to be one step ahead of her. What had she told him? She doubted Finn's grandfather had spoken a single word, as the man rarely seemed to care one way or another. He did, however, stanchly support whatever his wife deemed important.

"I do work, Laird. My son, Finn, has never gone hungry."

"Is it true he steals food from the village vendors?"

"He is mischievous as most ten-year-old lads are. Does it for fun, not because he is hungry."

The laird studied her, his attention not wavering. Robena knew she'd lose the fight for her son if she didn't come up with a way to convince the laird. But nothing came to mind.

"Missus Mackay, I do not see how living with ye instead of a well-established family which, to my knowledge, had been the boy's primary caregiver since birth would benefit him." The laird's gaze softened upon meeting hers. "I will order that ye be allowed to live there at the home. That way ye can be part of the boy's life."

He turned away to look at a young man, who she assumed was his scribe. "Write a missive directing that the Mackays allow Robena Mackay to live at the family home and treated as a member of the family."

"I do not wish to live there," Robena started.

"I am a father, and I would do even the most unpleasant things to ensure to be near my son. I suspect ye would as well."

He motioned to another person, promptly dismissing her. When Robena turned to walk away, she was shocked at how many people had entered and waited for their turn. While speaking to the laird, she had felt as if she was the only one in the room. Despite the fact things had not gone her way, she had to admire the way he took the time to ensure to give her all his attention.

The squire informed her the signed missive would not be available until later that day or the next, his attention flitting between her and the laird. "Ye are staying here, are ye not?"

"Aye," she replied, doing her best to keep from crying. "I am."

"I will find ye." The young man gave her an understanding look. "I will add that ye can go for visits away from the home with yer son. I am sure the laird will not have a problem with it."

"Thank ye." She dashed away in the direction of her small bedchamber, but instead kept walking until she found herself outside.

BY EARLY AFTERNOON, the mists of the early morning had dissipated giving a clearer view of the mountain side. Sheep grazed contently on the green grasses along the flatter ground, while more adventurous goats stood on steep ledges seeming to dare one another to climb higher.

Her gaze traveled to a field which had been set up for guards to practice sword play. There were only a few who sparred, while a few more shot with bows, their arrows hitting the targets with steady accuracy.

It seemed life at the keep was steady and constant. However, she suspected things were ever changing.

A tall, dark-haired man walked closer and met her gaze. By his dress and the fact a sword was strapped to his back, he was a warrior. Well built, with the rugged look and flat gaze she'd come to recognize meant he'd been to battle.

"Ye should not be on this side of the building unless accompanied." His dark gaze moved from her to the doorway. "Many of my men are not polite in the presence of women."

So, he was a leader. Upon closer inspection, he was less rugged, and a bit refined in looks. With dark brown waves that fell to his shoulders and thickly lashed eyes of the same color, he was quite handsome.

"I did not know." Robena sighed. "Where can I go to get fresh air and be out of the way?"

Just then about ten men appeared. All heavily armed and probably about to start practicing.

"Come," he said taking her elbow.

"I am Torac Mackinnon," he said by way of introduction. "I will show you a better place to get time alone."

For some reason she felt at ease with him. He was serious of demeanor, but at the same time something about him gave her a sense of being protected.

"I am Robena Mackay. I came to speak to the laird."

Torac nodded. "I am aware. I was in the party that went to yer village."

They came to an area that was walled in. It allowed for her to see the practice field but would be far enough to not be bothered by the men. Overhead, a wooden canopy had been built to shield from the sun and rain. There were several chairs and benches and a pair of tables.

"This is where the keep servants come to rest or to watch the guard's practice if they wish," Torac explained.

Robena met his gaze. "Can I ask ye something?"

He nodded.

"Is it possible to change the laird's mind once he makes a decision?"

"Our laird is a good and fair leader. I do not know what yer request is, but I suspect he made the best decision. Ye must think on it and perhaps find it is so." He looked past her and then to Robena again. "Be with care."

As he walked away, Finella appeared. "That Torac, he is quite handsome is he not?" She gave Robena a wide smile.

"He seems nice."

"His sister Cait is married to Stuart Ross, brother to the laird."

Robena considered that if she herself married, it was possible to change the laird's mind about her plight. Surely with the security of a husband who could support her and Finn, it would make things easier. However, at the moment, she had no suitors and if she were to be honest, no wish to marry so soon after her husband's death.

On the other hand, a husband would possibly be her best option. Choices for a suitable husband were limited at the village and perhaps here. Her gaze moved to where guards sparred as Torac looked on. Here at the keep were many men.

In addition, she could ask for work and find a way to get to know the laird better.

"What are ye thinking?" Finella asked. "Ye have not taken yer eyes off of Torac."

She started. "I am so sorry. Are ye and he…"

"Goodness no," Finella said, laughing. "I have my eyes on that one." She pointed to a pair of archers. "The one with the strap across his back. He is called Ivan and we are courting."

For a few moments, they watched the archers. Robena smiled at Finella. "He is very good. I cannot see his face since their backs are turned, but he has a fine form."

"Aye he does." A wide smile transformed Finella's face to one only a woman in love could display.

"I'd best get back. Lady Ross should be coming to give the daily talk at any moment."

Robena stood as well. "May I accompany ye? I will work while waiting for it to be time to return."

They walked into the small dining room beside the kitch-en. Two women she'd noticed earlier during midday meal were there. One was the laird's wife, Lady Isobel Ross, the other she assumed was his mother, Lady Mariel.

The laird's wife gave instructions to the chamber maids, the laundresses and to the cooks. She was efficient but friendly, often asking Gara or Lady Mariel questions to ensure nothing was missed.

"More visitors will be here until tomorrow. Ensure their bedchambers are refreshed, perhaps fresh flowers, and open the windows to air them out. Lady Mariel and I are taking the women to the village, so that gives ye plenty of opportunity to work. Do not touch any of their personal belongings if at all possible."

Lady Mariel gave instructions for the meals, then Gara spoke to the kitchen servants, giving each a different duty. Her gaze lighted on Robena for a moment. "Mister Artair has asked that ye not be assigned work duties."

Neither Lady Mariel nor Isobel seemed to think Artair's request strange.

The staff dispersed with their orders.

Robena tried to keep her voice even despite her nerves at addressing the laird's wife and mother. "I must ask for work while I remain here. I need coin and am willing to do whatever is needed."

"The chambermaids will need help," Finella interjected. "With the visitors and all."

Lady Isobel smiled. "I understand. Ye may help the chambermaids. However, I will speak to Artair to find out what he is expecting ye to do."

"Thank ye." She hurried out before the woman changed her mind.

The work turned out to be light. The chambermaids were fast and proficient, leaving Robena to make the beds as they swept, emptied bedpans, and dusted.

FINISHING UP ONE space, Robena pulled the bedding up and patted it in place.

"What are ye doing in my bedchamber?" The woman, Clara, hurried in and glared at her. "I will alert a guard immediately." She turned.

"I am working," Robena said in a flat voice. "As a chambermaid."

"Oh?" Clara turned slowly, her gaze traveling over Robena's dress and crisp white apron. "I see."

A strange transformation happened; it was as if the woman considered it the best news. "Carry on then. See about airing out my bedding and sweep out the fireplace."

The annoying woman then picked up a scarf and swept out of the room with a soft smile on her face. She was up to something. And whatever it was it had to do with Artair.

IT WAS JUST before last meal that Robena finished her chores. It was satisfying to do something and stay busy. While cleaning, she'd barely thought about Finn and the current situation.

The laundry was a bustle of activity when she entered. Lads rushed to and fro pulling wagons of water jugs.

Women scrubbed clothes while others hung the rinsed items up to dry on long ropes outside. The clean items flapped in the wind like proud banners.

Robena dropped off her basket and went to the kitchen to eat. As she walked past the great room, she noticed Torac standing by a doorway. Possibly he was working, though she wasn't sure.

When they made eye contact, he motioned for her to come closer.

"Have ye had any news?" he asked, and she was grateful to know someone cared enough to ask.

"Nothing new. I do not believe the laird will change his mind. I will try to speak to him again. Otherwise, I have to ponder if I should move in with my late husband's family."

She let out a breath. "I am not sure what to do. The scribe told me he will add to the missive that I be allowed to take my son away for visits."

Torac nodded in understanding. "I am sorry."

"Thank ye," Robena reached forward and touched his forearm. "It is kind of ye to say."

He nodded and turned his attention to the room, scanning it before looking to her. "If ye require anything, I am here."

When she turned and went to the corridor, Artair blocked her from passing. His gaze traveled past her to Torac and back before he spoke. "Why are ye dressed in such a manner?"

"I asked Lady Ross for work. I will be serving as chambermaid until we leave. I require coin and am glad to have a way to earn it."

Again, his gaze moved past her in the direction of where Torac stood. "Do ye know Torac?"

"I only met him since arriving." She wanted to tell him it was none of his business but decided against it. There was no reason for Artair to have any proprietary notions. She was not his or Torac's woman for that matter.

"Ye should not have to work while here. Ye are here as my guest."

Letting out a sigh, she lowered her gaze. "I have to do what I can to earn a living. Ye must understand it."

"Where are ye going now?" He motioned to the corridor. "I will walk with ye."

"There is no need . . ."

"I spoke with Darach. He seems to have a strong opinion of ye based on what yer late husband's mother told him. However, he may change his mind if we come up with a better way for ye to provide for him."

Robena stopped and looked at him. "There is little I can do

to change my circumstances."

They'd arrived at the kitchen. Gara came and looked up at Artair.

"How fares yer father?" asked Gara.

"Much better. I will see him in a pair of days."

The cook smiled. "I will send some tincture for him."

With one last look at Robena, Artair walked out the door to the courtyard, leaving her in the kitchen with Gara.

"Come and eat. Soon it will be time to prepare to serve last meal." Gara glanced after Artair. "That man needs to find out what his purpose is. Otherwise, he will continue to be restless, going from here to there."

"Has he always been like that?" Robena asked as she followed the woman into the small dining room.

Gara seemed to consider it, biting her bottom lip. "He has always had a strong opinion about things. When a wee lad, he pronounced he would become a warrior and conqueror." The woman chuckled. "Once a bit older, he proclaimed that he never wish to marry or have a woman control him, among other rather outlandish things."

Considering his personality in just the short time since she'd met him, it seemed to her as if he was set in his way of thinking. "Perhaps he is meant to be what he is now. A warrior who travels and lives where he is most needed."

"That lass, I do not believe. There is a look in his gaze akin to longing when he watches his cousins and their families. He is being foolish to think not to desire as much for himself."

There weren't as many people present in the great room for last meal. However, Robena offered to help serve. She carried a tray with mincemeat pies and dolled them out to those wishing for it.

When she neared the table where Lady Mariel sat, she noted the visiting woman Clara sat there. Robena reached to place a small platter of pies in the center of the table.

Something caught against her boot. The tray flew from her hands and skipped across the table, depositing small pies among the platters and mugs. Unable to catch herself, Robena landed face-down on the cold stone floor.

"My goodness, ye are a clumsy thing are ye not?" Clara said. She daintily sorted through the jumble of pies and finding one intact, took a bite.

Strong arms lifted Robena to her feet as a maid hurried over to restore order to the table. Torac's concerned gaze locked to her face.

Robena fought not to cry, but she was embarrassed, and the side of her head throbbed. "I am fine." Reaching to touch the side of her forehead, she cringed. It really hurt.

"What happened?" Artair came and stood in front of her, practically pushing Torac aside. "Are ye injured?"

"So much concern over a maid," Clara said, her voice dripping with sarcasm. "One would think she was important to ye."

Artair instantly dropped his hand from Robena's arm and stepped back. "I brought her here and wanted to ensure she is uninjured."

"It is obvious she is injured," Torac said in a flat voice.

For a moment no one moved or said anything. Robena blinked back tears and looked to Lady Mariel. "I am so sorry. I will strive to be more careful."

Lady Mariel nodded glancing between Torac and Artair.

"It was not yer fault. Go see Gara to ensure ye do not have too much bruising."

Torac walked with her to the kitchen. "That woman tripped ye."

"I know," Robena replied. "I do not know why she dislikes me so. I do not know her."

"It's obvious she hopes for a match with Artair Ross. Her family is here to find her a husband. It is also obvious he is attracted to ye."

Robena let out an exasperated huff. "Nothing will be between Artair and I. He is not a man to settle down with a family. I am sure Miss Clara will find out soon enough."

CHAPTER NINE

"THE MEN WERE tight-lipped, but once one broke and spoke, the others followed suit," Artair informed Darach. They were joined by Duncan and Erik, who wore an angry expression.

"They did not say anything we did not already know," Erik snapped. "Claim to be on their own, wanting to claim land for themselves."

Darach frowned. "It could be true. Since they are not from the Isles they must have considered our lands without rule."

"And then they fought to become rulers themselves," Artair added.

"What we need to find out is who their leader is," Duncan stated. "He may be one of the men we have."

They continued discussing what to do about the prisoners and finally concluded that the best action would be to continue to question and observe the men until they discovered the leader. Meanwhile, Artair would return to the southern post.

It suited him fine. It would give him the opportunity to visit again with his family without his brother being there.

According to guards who had arrived the day before, so far, all Bryce had done was refuse to work, and remained at the guard quarters. As annoying as it was, in a way, it would give his brother a broader view of what men with actual responsibilities did.

"Did Robena Mackay speak to ye?" Artair asked his cousin, hating the soft heat that rose to his face. Despite the fact he did not plan to spend time with the lass after depositing her back at the village, something about her stayed with him.

"How did ye come across this woman, Robena?" Darach asked. "It seems odd that she appears here just a few days after her deceased husband's mother, and with ye of all people."

"She was taken by those men. I'd met her before; her boy is the one who stole my clothes when I was bathing."

His cousin nodded. "I hear he has a habit of stealing."

It occurred to Artair that Darach seemed to have a bad opinion of Robena and how she handled the boy. In truth, he had no idea if Finn did any stealing before living with Robena. He would have to find out. "It seems to me the boy does it for sport."

"I do not agree with bairns being taken from their mother. In this case, however, he seems to have been raised away from her."

The air stilled a bit as a protective sensation surfaced. "We cannot assume to know what really happens unless everyone is present. I would think the boy has a different story to tell than either side you've heard."

"I will not force the Mackays to return the boy. He is better off there than with her. I will, however, send a missive ordering she be allowed to live there, if she so wishes. That way she can remain in the boy's life."

Artair could not believe his ears. Jumping to his feet he approached Darach. "She is the boy's mother. They cannot just take him. She is a widow."

"I am aware," Darach stated. "However, he was raised by his father's family and spent most of his life away from his mother. Ye must be aware that she cannot provide as stable a home for the lad."

Once Darach pointed out the obvious about Robena not having the security necessary to provide for the boy, Artair settled. It was the same thing he'd been thinking.

Robena had to be heartbroken.

"There is something ye should consider if ye care for the lass," Darach said, snatching his attention back.

"What?" Although Artair did not plan to be part of Robena's future, he was interested in what his cousin had to say.

"Marry her. With ye as a provider, I would change my mind and allow the lad to choose who to live with. However, if the lad prefers to remain with his grandparents, I will not force him otherwise."

"Marriage," Artair said, incredulous. "Ye are aware how I feel about it. I do not plan to ever marry. There is no need for it. I've always thought it an arrangement more for convenience than other reasons."

Erik laughed. "Most men do not consider marriage unless forced. Women have that effect on us, I suppose. I agree with Artair. There is no need for it."

They were silent for a moment. Finally Duncan stood, a rare grin on his face as if he knew a secret they didn't.

"Speaking of such, I must return to my wife and bairn." He met Artair's gaze. "Ye have always made clear announcements of what ye will and will not do. Ye should be with care cousin. Ye never know when fate decides it has had enough of it."

Despite the fact he chuckled as if it didn't matter, Artair

almost raced after Duncan to ask why he'd made the statement.

It was true, he did make bold statements. But usually it was because he wanted to be clear about things. As far as marriage was concerned, it had always felt distant to him. It held little attraction. A wife and children would only hinder his nomadic life.

Although his father planned for him to settle at the family's lands, he did not feel drawn to such a life. Several years earlier, he'd picked the area where he'd built a house and had the land cleared of trees. He'd done it when his father had been very ill, to assure his father he'd do his duty and return to the family lands.

However, he'd never moved forward on the build. Instead, Artair visited his parents often then returned to work on the northeastern part of the Isle.

A few months earlier, he'd returned to Keep Ross and now was to work at the southern post. It was only an effort to remain close to his father and help where he could without making the commitment of living on the family lands.

"I will seek out Robena and find out what she plans. I suspect she can return to the village when I head back in that direction."

Darach studied him. "Be sure you give my regards to Uncle Angus. I take it he is doing better."

"Yes, he is. However, I plan to go by there more often. Just to be sure he does not overdo things."

There were only a few people lingering in the great hall when he walked through. Servants swept the floors and scrubbed the tables in preparation for the next meal.

"Have ye seen Robena?" Artair asked at the kitchen doorway. "I cannot find her."

Finella, looked up from her task. "I believe Torac fetched her for a walk. Robena remains quite upset at my laird's decision."

His jaw clenched. Was Torac about to court Robena? Why else did the warrior come for her? "Where did they go?"

"I am not sure," Finella replied.

Artair went to the doorway and peered out to the courtyard, not seeing either Torac or Robena. He stalked out and went toward the guard practice field. It was empty. He then continued toward the stables. The couple was not there, either.

For whatever reason, anger surfaced. If Torac took advantage of a grieving woman, Artair'd confront the man.

Just then he spotted them. The pair walked from the gates and seemed to be deep in conversation. Robena carried a basket with flowers as she turned to glance at the warrior who'd said something.

They continued toward the back door he'd just walked through. Artair wanted to approach Robena, but instead remained still to watch.

She looked up at Torac and said something. There was sadness in her expression. She reached and touched the warrior's forearm, her hand lingering a moment.

With Torac turned away, Artair could not see the man's expression. The warrior must have been speaking because Robena continued to look up at him.

Then they went their separate ways. Torac turned toward the guard quarters and Robena continued inside. Artair hurried across the courtyard, torn as to whether to follow the warrior or speak to Robena.

He chose Robena.

"Darach told me what he decided. I am very sorry," he said by way of greeting. "I should have been there to help ye."

Robena's gaze moved to meet his. "It is not yer battle, but mine. I did as much as I could. Unfortunately, my husband's mother arrived earlier to plead her case."

"What can I do?"

When she looked to him, she seemed sad and uncertain. "I do not think anything can be done."

"There must be."

When Artair took a step closer, she moved away. Not much, but enough that he caught the movement.

"I best go inside. Lady Mariel requested flowers in the guest's bedchambers."

"Ye do not have to work while ye are here."

There was a soft lift to the corners of her lips. "As I informed ye before, I require coin. Therefore, this is a perfect opportunity to be paid and earn money for later."

He remained still as she walked into the house. It was best that he distance himself. Surely Robena felt a stronger tie to someone like Torac. Not that he considered himself above her in social status—truth be told, he and she were from the same background. Their fathers owned land and animals.

Robena, however, had been left with only a small plot of land and a small cottage because her husband was supposed to be the one who supported her. It proved unfortunate that both her husband and parents died at the same time.

THAT EVENING, ARTAIR decided to retire early. There wasn't much to do, and he needed time to think about how to help Robena.

"Ah there ye are." Clara waited in the corridor outside his

bedchamber. It was not the first time a woman hoped to gain his attention pretending to be seeking him near his bedchamber. When she looked to the door, it was obvious she expected to be invited inside.

Artair observed her. She was an attractive woman, the type he did not mind taking to bed. However, in this case, her family was here for a prolonged visit, and he suspected it was to find her a compatible husband.

He forced a pleasant expression despite the fact he'd been looking forward to time alone. This was most inopportune.

"Miss Clara," Artair murmured, lifting her hand to his lips. "Is there something that troubles ye?"

He took her elbow and guided her toward the end of the corridor where they could look out to the courtyard. She frowned. Obviously, she'd planned on him being more than willing to invite her inside his bedchamber.

"I am a bit tired. Is there somewhere we can sit and talk?"

There weren't any chairs or benches on the balcony, so he was at a loss.

"I can escort ye to yer bedchamber if ye are tired."

At this, her lips curved. "That would be most gallant of ye. I do find myself a bit winded from the activities of the day." She slid her arm through his. "I hear ye are to return to the southern portion of the lands. When will that be?"

"As soon as possible. I have much to do."

"My home is not too far from yer parents. Were ye aware that our fathers are friendly?"

He was not. Since he'd left at a young age to squire for the late laird and since he only returned home on occasion, Artair did not know many of his father's acquaintances.

It was something he had to rectify.

"I thought to have met yer father before. However, I believe it was here during one of his yearly visits."

She smiled up at him and leaned closer. "Ye were not here the last time I visited. A pity. I would have loved for us to have spent time together."

The offer, however tempting it should have been, had the opposite effect. Something about the woman made him think of a sly creature which lurks in the darkness waiting for unsuspecting prey. Instead of attraction, he felt nothing.

He let out a breath when they reached her bedchamber door. "Ah, here we are. Assure ye get plenty of rest." He opened the door, gently pushed her inside, then closed it firmly.

If anyone would have seen him dash from there, they would have thought him frightened. It was possible he was.

He hurried back down the stairs and through the great room. Artair approached the first person he found and tapped their shoulder. "Where is the woman, Robena?"

The maid smiled. "She's gone to her bedchamber, Mister Artair."

It was becoming late, but it was imperative he spoke to her.

After a rap on the door, she called out permission to enter. Artair looked over his shoulder and caught sight of the woman, Clara, going down the stairs.

He opened the door, hurried in, and slammed the panel shut behind him.

Robena's eyes widened, obviously not expecting him. "I thought ye were Finella . . ." She looked past him to the closed door. "This is most inappropriate."

"I know," Artair said. "I apologize. It is just that I have to inform ye we leave first thing in the morning. I must go see my father."

A slight frown marred her brow. "I have barely begun to work. I thought we were to remain at least another sennight."

Making quick work of untying his purse from his belt, he handed it to her. "Here. Take this."

She held up the heavy purse, giving him an incredulous look. "This is too much. I have barely worked one day."

"Isobel is very impressed with yer work. Now please pack yer things and meet me in the courtyard at dawn." He turned to walk out but stopped at the thought of Clara looking for him.

He cracked the door just a bit, peeked out, then closed it. Turning back around, he met Robena's gaze. "Would ye mind looking out and telling me who is about?"

"What is the matter with ye? Ye are acting so strange." She shoved the purse back at him, but he kept his arms to his sides.

With a sigh, she placed the bag on a small table and went to the door. Opening it, she stepped out and peered toward the great room.

"Who do ye see?" Artair whispered.

Her lips curved. "That woman Clara seems to be asking a maid something."

Standing in the corridor, Robena crossed her arms. "Ye should move away from the door," she whispered. "She is coming this way."

Just then he heard Clara's unmistakable high-pitched voice. "Have ye seen Mister Artair?"

"Aye, Miss Clara, he stopped by to give me instructions."

There was a pause. "Did he tell ye where he was going?"

"A Ross has no reason to inform me of anything," Robena said. "If I were to guess, he was going to relieve himself. He seemed rather unwell. A strained look about him."

It was obvious Robena tried to keep from smiling when she walked back into the room, shutting the door. "Ye should leave."

The last thing he wanted was to be found in some sort of compromising way with Clara, who obviously had a plan in mind and would not be put off. She must have gone back to his bedchamber and found him gone.

Looking about the room, he noted there were two beds. "I will sleep here. That way in the morning I can assure ye will be ready."

"Ye will do no such thing," Robena said.

"Lower yer voice," he hissed. "The woman might hear ye."

"It is not me she is searching for."

Both jumped when there was another rap on the door. This time Robena opened it.

It was Finella.

"In the morning, Gara requests . . ." The maid's eyes widened. "Mister Artair. Miss Clara is looking for ye."

He hurried to the door, pulled Finella inside and closed the door. "Do not tell her I am here."

"Finella, can I sleep in yer room? Mister Artair seems to think he can hide here with me all night."

To his consternation Finella burst out laughing. "It is not the first time a Ross hides in our chambers. Unfortunately, I do not have an extra bed, I'm afraid. I am sure Mister Artair will stay in his own bed."

"We leave in the morning, first thing," Robena told her.

Finella frowned and gave Robena a quick hug. "I have

enjoyed meeting ye. I will tell mother and we will have food packed for ye both."

Artair removed his boots and climbed onto the bed. He crossed his arms across his chest. "How do people sleep on these narrow things? I am not sure."

For a long moment Robena glared at him. "I must undress. Please turn away." When he did, she murmured. "Ye expect a lot in return for helping me. First, I share a bedchamber with ye and yer brother and now ye again. This is most unseemly."

He couldn't help but smile. A woman like her, who spoke her mind and showed such strength, was admirable. The sounds of fabric shifting and finally the room going dark meant he could roll to his back. Artair almost fell from the bed . . . more of a cot if he were to be honest.

"I have not gotten the missive from yer cousin," Robena said.

"I will retrieve it in the morning. I believe the scribe had him sign it today."

"I am not sure what to do. The Mackays will not be happy about the laird's direction that I must live there."

Artair understood she was in a hurry to see her son. "I can take ye there first and then be on my way to my family's home."

There was a long silence. "Will ye remain for a bit please? I do not trust them not to kick me out as soon as ye leave."

"I will inform them that our guards will be stopping by on occasion."

Her shaky breath sounded. "Why are ye hiding from Miss Clara?"

"Her family is set on finding her a husband and she's set her sights on me."

"Ye are against marriage, then?"

"Not for some people. My parents for example. I am glad they married."

To his surprise, Robena giggled. It was a sweet musical sound. "I am sure when the right woman comes along, ye will change yer mind."

"Hmm," he replied.

AT DAWN THE following morning Artair hurried into the kitchen. When he woke, Robena was already gone from the room, as was her small bundle. After retrieving the missive from the scribe, he found the bundle in the kitchen, but not Robena.

"Where is Robena?" he asked Finella, who was ladling porridge into bowls.

"She went to tell Torac she is leaving."

Gritting his teeth, he went to the door and peered out. They stood by the well. Not close, but a respectable distance. Robena said something and Torac nodded. Then she turned and hurried toward where Artair stood.

Artair wondered if by taking her away he was interrupting what would be a good match for her. If he remembered correctly, Torac was to be assigned to the southern post soon.

When she neared and her gaze met his, the dark brown pools taking him in, Artair could not help touching her. He reached for her shoulder and slid his hand over the curve of it. "Are ye ready?"

She nodded. "Aye."

His horse was brought out from the stables. The giant war horse's head bobbed as it anticipated the upcoming travel.

"Very well."

CHAPTER TEN

THEY RODE FOR a long while before stopping. Artair was unusually silent, which Robena was glad for. Her mind was a tumble between the thought of seeing Finn again and feeling so strangely about the two men in her life, Torac and Artair.

Torac was strong in his silence, most of his communication coming from the way he looked at her. He'd told her he was to be at the southern post soon for many months and would come and see about her. There was something about him that attracted her. And, in a way, she considered they would be a good match. She did find him attractive, although her body did not react to him. With his close connection to Clan Ross, as his wife she could fight for the laird to change his ruling.

Then there was Artair. Whenever he was near, her pulse raced, and it was difficult to breathe normally. The way he touched her and had kissed her was as if they'd known each other forever. And although her body reacted strongly to him, she still felt comfortable in his presence.

The man had made it more than clear he had no desire to ever settle, so she constantly reminded herself it was best not to pin any hopes on something developing between them.

"We will have to spend the night somewhere," Artair told

her, glancing at the sky. "It is about to storm."

As if on cue, the first drops of rain began falling. They'd been traveling for half a day and Robena was exhausted, hungry, and desperately needed to stretch her legs. So, upon coming to a small village, she was grateful for the break.

The couple who owned a small tavern had rented out the only room they had, but were gracious and offered up their own bedchamber. The tavern-keeper's wife, a bubbly woman, served them a delicious hot meal.

Robena wanted to inform everyone they would not share a bed, but she was too overwhelmed to argue with Artair. The closer they got to Taernsby, the more a sense of foreboding took over. She was on the verge of tears by the time they retired to the bedchamber.

The room was tidy and of a good size. The woman had changed the linens and opened the window to freshen up the space.

"I will wait outside for ye to get ready for bed." Artair walked out.

Robena quickly undressed to her chemise. She went to the window and peered out. The view of mostly trees with a single road cutting through was pretty. It would be the road she and Artair would take the next day.

When he walked in, she turned.

"Why are ye crying?" He neared and took her face with both hands.

She'd not realized she was so upset. "I do not know. I feel . . . sad."

He pressed kisses to her wet cheeks, brushing away each tear. A sweeter thing she'd never experienced before. It felt natural when his mouth took hers, gently kissing her lips. The longer the kiss continued, the more she didn't wish it to ever end.

To be lost in him was a salve to her tattered spirit. "Artair," she whispered and wrapped her arms around his neck. "I need ye."

His breath caught at the unexpected request, and he pulled her against his large body. His hands slid down her back and back up.

The most wonderful sensations like the sinful comfort of sinking into a hot bath rolled over her body. She wanted to crawl into him and remain there forever. It was as if Artair spun a protective web around them.

He carried her to the bed, placed her on it gently, and quickly removed his clothes. Artair had a striking physique. So strong and muscled, while at the same time lean.

When he came over her, she could only sigh as his weight crushed down. Once again, he took her mouth. His hands slid up under her chemise, the rough pads of his fingertips skimming up her overly sensitive skin.

"Ye are so beautiful," he whispered in her ear. "I wish to kiss every inch of yer body."

Rolling to his back, he pulled her astride his hips and pulled her chemise up, tugging it from beneath her bottom, past her waist, and finally over her head. He drew her down to lie atop him.

The coolness of the room swept over her exposed skin and she shivered. The clothing was replaced by his warm hands which caressed from her upper legs over her bottom and up her back. All the while he kissed her neck, his lips trailing over the skin, barely seeming to touch it.

Robena ran her hands down his sides to his hips, the warm skin sending tendrils of want that pooled between her legs. She lifted her face to him, and he took her mouth again, this time with rugged passion, their teeth clashing.

He chuckled and nibbled at her bottom lip. "Sorry."

Then, he rolled her on her back and took her mouth properly, suckling at her lips, delving past them with his tongue while his hands caressed her breasts.

Robena was lost, gone to a wonderful place filled with heat, passion, and stars which burst into bright formations.

It was not enough. She needed to be completely and utterly lost. Robena raked her fingers through his hair and lifted her hips, demanding to be taken.

Seeming to understand this was not a time for gentle lovemaking, Artair thrust into her and she moaned loudly. Each movement fanned the flames of want, until her entire body was consumed by the wonderful heat.

"Please more," she demanded huskily. "More."

Lifting up to his elbows so he could look down at her, Artair rocked his hips, moving in and out of her in a steady rhythm.

The intensity of his expression was raw and sensual as he concentrated on his movements. He pulled out and plunged back in, each thrust sending Robena closer to losing all control. Her fingers dug into his hips as she urged him on.

Closing her eyes, she concentrated on every sensation. The sounds of their breathing and his gruff moans, their bodies moving in unison, skin hitting skin, and even the soft crackles of the fire.

As if the world stood still for them, all that she could think about was the next moment.

Artair moved faster, his lunges harder, and Robena could no longer control her reactions. Her cries of rapture echoed in her ears as the surroundings faded and her entire body was consumed with a sweet heat that sent her free-falling.

"Oh!" She cried as her sex tightened around his. Artair moaned loudly and shuddered. In an instant all went black and she could not tell if she fell or soared. There were no words to describe the experience. So many sensations, emotions, and sounds assailed at once and all she could do was pray it did not end.

Moments, later, Artair pulled her against his side and pressed a kiss to her temple. Both were silent.

Neither knew what to say. The moment had been purely physical, no promises, no commitments. At the same time, she'd never felt closer to someone than to Artair in that moment. It struck her as strange to feel so close to another person and yet there were no expectations.

It was probably her need to feel protected and close to someone after so many months of being alone, with no one to lean on, that had allowed the freedom to give herself to the moment.

There were no illusions on her part that he felt the same as she in that moment. She looked at him and he pulled her closer.

She turned Artair's face and pressed a soft kiss on his lips. "Sleep well."

Then she rolled to her side and gently pushed his arm out of the way so they no longer touched.

There was no sense of loss. In fact, feeling his body heat was comforting and she fell asleep quickly.

THE NEXT MORNING after breaking their fast, Robena felt refreshed and ready to face her late husband's family. She donned a clean dress and brushed her hair, braiding it and rolling it into a tight bun at her nape.

Artair gave her an appreciative look when she came down the stairs. The tavern owner's wife smiled widely. "Ye are a very attractive couple. Yer bairns will be lovely."

When Artair cleared his throat, seeming unable to find words, Robena strolled closer to the woman. "How nice of ye to say. The bedroom was quite comfortable. Thank ye for allowing us to stay."

The woman grinned. "I am glad."

They ate breakfast and Robena reached for Artair's forearm. "I appreciate ye accompanying me to the Mackay's home. I am not sure what my reception would be if I appeared alone."

"I will not allow for any mistreatment and will ensure they are aware ye have the laird's and my protection." When he met her gaze there seemed to be a hint of uncertainty lurking in her eyes. "Is there anything else ye require?"

Robena thought for a long moment. unsure if there was anything she was forgetting. "I will have one of the men who work there accompany me to get my things from the cottage. I considered selling it, but first I must see what Finn thinks. When he gets older, I may want to move away."

There was a flicker in his gaze, and she knew he was surprised at her lack of demands after what had occurred between them.

Once they finished eating and Artair paid the tavern owners more than they asked for, they walked out to find the horse.

She eyed the hard saddle askance, uncertain of sitting astride. It had been a long time since she'd been with a man, and it had been the first time she'd enjoyed bedsport for as long as she and Artair had.

"Is something wrong?" he asked coming up behind her, preparing to help her to mount.

Robena looked around, her cheeks heating. "I do not think I can sit astride comfortably today."

For a scant moment Artair seemed not to understand and then his brows came together. He cleared his throat. "Of course. I understand. Ye can ride with yer legs to one side."

Once she was settled sideways, he mounted and held her between his arms. Robena decided she'd rather be sore than sit that way. Not only did it feel awkward, but her face was practically against his.

"Are ye in pain?"

Her face reddened and she looked to her left away from him. "I am fine."

They rode for a few hours before they finally neared the village. Artair stopped at a clearing so they could relieve themselves. He stood by the horse when Robena emerged from the woods.

His hair was to his shoulders, the waves blowing sideways past his face. Wearing a gray tunic and black breeches, he looked quite dashing. Her heart skipped a beat.

He grasped her shoulders. "Robena, last night was like no

other for me. I wish ye to know that I care for ye."

The words brought a warmth, her heart demanded she ask to stay with him. "Ye have given me what I needed most. To feel close to someone, and not so alone in the world. I will never forget ye."

A confused expression crossed his features, but then he gave her a tight smile and nodded. "We should get on then."

When he put his hands on her waist and lifted her, their gazes locked. Robena wasn't sure if she kissed him or the other way around, but moments later they were kissing until breathless, clinging to one another as if they were the last two humans left in the world.

Somehow, they managed to break apart. Robena's body protested, demanding more. She walked a few steps away and blew out several slow breaths.

When she returned, Artair lifted her to the horse. This time she chose to ride astride. Immediately she was aware of his arousal, which did little to settle hers.

The house looked and felt foreboding. So different than when she first arrived. Newly married to a man she'd been infatuated with, Robena had only seen the illusion. At barely sixteen, she'd felt like the luckiest girl in the village.

Her husband had been older than her by ten years and attractive. But Matthew Mackay was cruel, taking joy from each way he stripped Robena of every ounce of self-assurance, until shattering her to pieces. First, by his rough manner at lovemaking, often leaving her bruised and sore. Then by humiliating her in front of his family and friends. Finally, he'd taken their son at merely a few months of age and, along with another woman, had traveled for months on end.

Over the extent of their marriage, she was glad he took lovers, because that meant he would ignore her. What she hated was that her son saw her less and less as Finn was taken on trips by either her husband or his family.

A man hurried to greet them. His guarded expression changed upon recognizing her. "Miss Robena, how nice to see ye."

The man, the groundskeeper, had always been kind to her.

"Hello Rob. Are the Mackays here?"

He gave her a confused look. "Nay, they have been gone for several days. The house is closed as they plan to sell the property."

It was as if the earth shifted under her feet and although she knew the answer, the question had to be asked. "And Finn?"

"They and the boy all left. Even took most of the staff."

"Where have they gone? Exactly when did they leave?" Artair asked, taking her arm as if sensing she was about to collapse.

Rob looked at Artair. "Ye are a Ross are ye not?"

Artair nodded.

"They left four days ago. I believe to northern Scotland where the Mackay clan lives. They have family there."

Without a word, Robena turned and raced to the house. She burst through the front door and rushed through every room. The furniture was draped with large cloths, giving it the eerie look of abandonment.

Bursting through each door, she kept expecting to enter a room and find Finn. Her son could *not* be gone. Life could *not* be that cruel.

Upon entering Finn's bedchamber, she noticed the room was left without draping for some reason. His belongings were gone. The clothes, his toys and even the blanket she'd made for him. She caught sight of something peeking from beneath the bed. Her feet heavy as bricks, she walked closer and pulled it out. It was one of his tunics, the item still dirty from whatever he'd done that day. A sob escaped and she held it up to her cheek.

In her heart, she knew that if she ever saw Finn again, it would be many years from that day.

When she returned to the front room, Artair held out an envelope. "This was here on the table. I suspect they expected ye to come."

The sharp handwriting very familiar.

Robena,

I find it best that Finn be raised by his clan. Therefore, we have moved to Scourie, where he can join Clan Mackay. Ye must accept it is what is best for him.

The house has been sold, so ye cannot remain here.

Elena Mackay

Robena felt no emotion at reading the words. It was not a surprising message, but one that changed her future. Now she had no idea what to do, where to go.

Without a word, the missive crumpled in one hand and Finn's tunic in the other, she walked out, her gaze immediately turning to the sea.

"I am sorry." Artair came to stand next to her. "Fate has not been kind to ye."

Exhaustion overtook her and all Robena wanted was to sleep. "Will ye take me to my cottage, please?"

"I have to see about my father. I will bring ye with me there. Ye can rest and do as ye wish. The house is very large and ye can expect privacy."

There was no doubt that left to her own devices Robena would not care to live or die. Artair surely expected that to be the case and thus why he insisted to bring her to his family home. It mattered naught to her one way or the other, so she nodded in agreement.

CHAPTER ELEVEN

"WHAT HAPPENED TO the poor lass? I have never seen a more desolate creature in my life!" Artair's mother whispered even though Robena was in a room on the other side of the house.

He wasn't sure how to formulate everything that had occurred to Robena. When he considered it, the list was not long, but very sad.

"She lost her husband and parents. They drowned at sea when their bìrlinn overturned. Now her late husband's parents left the Isle and took Robena's young son with them."

His mother, Iona, always soft-hearted, lifted her hand and splayed it over her chest, an expression of complete sadness. "How dreadful. She must be torn to pieces."

"Aye, which is why I was reluctant to leave her alone at her cottage. She has no desire to live."

Footfalls neared and he was not surprised when Bryce walked in. "Ah, brother, I was not aware ye were here," he said in a light tone. "What brings ye?"

Having to grit his teeth to keep from raising his voice, Artair met his brother's gaze. "It should be me asking the question. Ye were to remain at the southern post."

"There is nothing to do there. Ride about and stare at trees. The guards act as if they're on a quest of huge importance, only to return and talk about how they found nothing. Then they sleep and repeat the process. What an utter waste of time."

"What is a waste is ye. Ye have absolutely no purpose. There was an attack, people were killed, we fought a pair of battles, men took a woman whom the guards rescued. How can ye say nothing happened?"

Bryce shrugged. "That was but a few days. Besides, I have to see about Isla and her bairn."

This time their mother became angered. "Ye mean *yer* bairn. It is not only she who produced the child. Sometimes, I have no more patience for ye Bryce."

"Ye need to work to support yer family." Artair met Bryce's flat gaze.

"And do what? I have no skills."

It was inconceivable that he and his brother were from the same parents. Bryce had no ambition or care to what happened around him. He was the most self-centered man Artair had ever met. It included McInerny, who wished to kill his way up to being laird.

Obviously, their mother had enough. She stood and leaned over her youngest son. "Ye must come up with a resolution and soon. Ye cannot be spending every waking moment locked up in a room doing whatever it is ye do."

"Did I not just say I was to see about it?" Bryce replied with annoyance. "I am not sure though what the best plan of action is."

"Find work, support yer family. Those are the first things that come to mind," Artair snapped.

Bryce narrowed his eyes. "I have no talents that would earn

me coin. I cannot magically make skills appear."

At the true statement everyone was silent.

"Can ye wield a sword or shoot arrows?" Artair asked.

"No and not since a child. Therefore, I doubt my archery skills have improved." Bryce studied his fingernails. "I can garden."

Artair blew out a hard breath. "No one pays someone to garden."

"I can paint, and I have dabbled a bit with numbers."

Iona looked up to the ceiling as if searching for answers. "Ye painted once, and I have never seen ye help yer father with the ledgers."

Bryce stood and stalked to a window. "Isla, the bairn, and I will live with ye and father."

Reluctantly, Artair had to agree. It was the best solution. "I agree, but on one condition."

"What is that brother?"

"That ye work with father. Take over some of the tasks. Ride the lands with him, get to know the farmers and their needs. Each day, ye must leave the house and do something other than dawdle and write poetry or whatever it is ye do."

"I have a condition as well," Iona said. "Ye must treat the lass and bairn well."

Bryce's expression became pensive. He met Artair's gaze. "I agree." He then looked to his mother. "I have never once mistreated a woman. My son will be cared for."

As if realizing something, Bryce studied him for a long moment. "Why did ye bring the woman here?"

A maid appeared at the door. "Last meal is ready."

"I will fetch Robena. She may wish to eat with us."

"Robena." Bryce met his gaze. "Pretty name. Are she and ye lovers?"

"Shut up Bryce," Artair replied, wishing he could punch his brother in the stomach.

"I MUST GO to last meal. I have to thank yer parents for allowing me be a guest," Robena said, surprising him. "Am I dressed well enough?"

She was perfect in his opinion; the cream-colored blouse complimented her olive skin perfectly. Along with it, she wore dark brown skirts and a matching shawl over her shoulders.

"Ye are." Artair took her elbow. "We are informal for our meals when not hosting."

Realizing what he said, Artair immediately cleared his throat. "I mean hosting large groups and such."

"I understood," Robena replied. "I am glad there isn't anything different planned in my behalf."

Upon entering the dining room, Artair was not surprised to find his parents alone, each on one end of a table that sat ten.

"Is Bryce delayed due to having to change his wardrobe?" He asked dryly. His father chortled and his mother gave him a bland look.

"How are ye dear?" She motioned for Robena to sit next to her. After holding out her chair and getting her settled, Artair took his seat on his father's right.

Just as he sat, Bryce entered with a young woman who blushed prettily upon meeting his gaze.

"This is Isla," Bryce said by way of introduction, looking to Robena.

"You've met my brother, Artair." He motioned to Artair, then walked to sit across from him.

Isla seemed taken back, unsure where to sit.

Artair stood, strolled to the opposite side of the table where Robena sat, and pulled out a chair for Isla. "Ye must excuse my brother. It has only been a short time since we allowed him out of the pen where he was raised with the hogs."

"Thank ye," Isla said, sliding a questioning look to Bryce who huffed and rolled his eyes.

Their father however, found Artair's comment humorous and laughed loudly. "Hog's pen!" he barked and laughed again.

When his mother giggled, Robena and Isla exchanged a look of uncertainty. Robena's lips lifted just a bit and, unable to keep laughter at bay, Isla chuckled.

"Thank God," Bryce said when two maids walked in to serve them.

ROBENA IMMEDIATELY LIKED both Iona and Isla. Both were warm in their greetings, and it seemed that Isla had only recently come to live there, so she was not yet comfortable with the family interactions.

From what she could tell, Artair and his father were much closer than the father and the younger son, Bryce.

Bryce Ross did not look one bit like Artair. His eyes were dark brown, as was his hair. He was good looking, shorter and slimmer than Artair, and had a boyish look about him. She wondered how old he was.

By contrast, Angus Ross and his son were built like warriors. The older man looked more like a warrior than a landowner. Robena mused that he must have been both as he was the late laird's brother. Despite having been very ill, he seemed healthy at the moment and with a robust appetite.

The man had greeted her earlier upon their arrival. Both he and Artair's mother immediately insisted she remain as long as she wished, even if Artair left to return to the southern post.

The bedchamber they'd given her was a bright room with a view of the garden and fields. She wasn't sure where Artair's chamber was, but she hoped not too far as she wasn't sure how her first night with the knowledge Finn was gone would go.

At thinking about Finn, her stomach clenched. The food was delicious, but it lost its appeal when measured against her grief.

"Ye should eat. It will help ye remain strong. If there is a way to find yer son, ye will want to be healthy enough to travel," Iona told her.

Isla met her gaze. "I will help ye with whatever ye need." The young woman was kind enough not to ask details and Robena was grateful.

"I appreciate it. However, I do not think anything can be done. If ever I see my son again, it will be when he decides to find me. Which may be years from now."

A tear slipped down her cheek and she wiped it away. "The food is indeed delicious." She lifted the spoon and ate a bit of the stew.

Isla and Iona exchanged looks and Artair's mother

changed the subject. “Isla, perhaps while Robena is here, we can take advantage of her skills and make some blankets for the bairn.”

They began speaking about what was needed, while Robena did her best to act interested. What she really wanted was to return to her bedchamber and sleep.

She and Artair were to remain for at least a sennight, and she was glad for it. Once they returned to the village, she had to formulate a plan for the future. She did not wish to leave so that when Finn finally came, it would be easier for him to find her.

A thought occurred. With new residents at the McKay house, she could possibly seek a position there. That would be one step closer to Finn finding her.

“If ye are finished, would ye like to go for a walk and get some fresh air before seeking yer bed?”

Artair, ever attentive, lowered to the chair next to hers. Bryce had finished eating and left. Isla and Iona continued discussing infant clothing and the patriarch asked for ale and a sweet tart to be brought to the sitting room.

“I would like that,” Robena said, glad to be away from the talk about bairns. Although she did love children, she did not particularly enjoy sewing or needlework.

A freshness of night air greeted as they stepped out through the front door. Artair took her hand. “Come, I wish to show ye something.”

It baffled her how at ease they were around each other. Artair seemed distant from most people from what she’d noticed, but with her, he was very demonstrative. It was always little touches, like a hand on the small of her back, taking her elbow, and now her hand.

They walked a short distance to the edge of a pond. Ducks glided effortlessly across the water to their shelters which looked like mounds of grass.

"They have homes," she exclaimed with a smile. "How sweet."

"Aye, father and I built the domed little structures on the water's edge for mother, who wanted the ducks to be safe from the elements. We were surprised the creatures actually use them."

They lowered to a bench and as soon as he sat next to her, Artair's arm came around her shoulders. "How are ye feeling?"

He was the most caring man. Of course, they would eventually go their separate ways and she did worry how she'd feel when it happened. For the moment however, she let out a sigh and leaned against his side.

"I feel . . . lost. It is as if I have no purpose or direction. However, an idea came to me."

He turned his head and pressed a kiss to her temple. "What is this idea?"

"To return to the Mackay house and ask the new owners to give me work there. It will be easier for Finn to find me when he returns."

Artair was silent for a beat. "As a servant?"

"I can cook, be a chambermaid or laundress. I do not mind work. This will afford me meals and a roof over my head. I have the cottage where I can go to rest."

Of course, Artair had no say in what she would do. They did not have that type of a relationship. He brought her there only because if left alone and she perished, he would feel responsible.

Noble to the end, he took his role of protecting people to heart.

"Yer brother is very different from ye," she said, needing to change the topic.

With a deep chuckle he shook his head. "Indeed, he is. I often wonder if he wasn't found somewhere by my parents and not truly a member of our family."

"Ye enjoy teasing him," Robena said. "He seems young."

"He is only five years younger. I am six and thirty. Bryce is one and thirty. He is not as young as he acts."

"And neither of ye have married until now, since Bryce will marry Isla."

"Bryce would not have married if not forced to because of Isla's condition. I do not plan to ever marry. Do not see a need for it."

Despite having accepted there was no future between them, his words made her chest tighten. She had to get away from Artair. The sooner the better. The last thing she needed was another devastating loss if she allowed her heart to become more involved than it already was.

"I am very tired. I wish to rest."

They stood and this time he didn't take her hand. Walking side-by-side in silence, she slid a look to him. His gaze forward, he seemed to be deep in thought.

He stopped abruptly and turned to her. "Robena. I hope to not have led ye to believe there would be more between us."

"I believe ye to be a very noble man and appreciate the extra care ye have taken. I do not expect anything more than to return to my village in a few days." Robena met his gaze.

"There is little I expect any more. It would be rather stupid of me after all that has happened."

Robena leaned in and hugged Artair, her body immediately alert at the feel of his muscular one against hers.

"Thank ye for everything." She quickly disengaged and hurried inside.

The next days passed quickly and Robena got into a routine of taking walks with Isla. She came to like the young woman and they could talk for hours. Isla confided not caring for Bryce's manner and hoped he would mature. Despite her annoyance, it was obvious she was taken with him and excited at the prospect of becoming a mother.

Robena on the other hand, shared about Finn and her life prior to the deaths of her husband and parents. When Isla asked about her relationship with Artair, she was honest and told her how comfortable they were together but insisted she did not expect to see him again once she returned to the village.

It rang true. There was no reason for her to see Artair again. However, at saying it, there was a twinge of pain that was enough to warn her against spending too much time alone with him.

One afternoon, when Artair announced they were to leave and return to the village, Robena asked him if they could use a cart. At first, he didn't seem to understand her reasoning.

"Is something wrong? Do ye feel unwell?"

She did not wish to ride close to him. It would make things harder upon arriving to the village. However, he would not agree to it unless she made up a good reason.

"My back has been bothering me," she said, keeping her

gaze averted. Truly, she was a horrible liar. Heat crept to her cheeks, and she swallowed past dryness that formed in her throat.

Artair looked through the window toward the stables. "Father, could I use one of yer wagons?"

"As long as ye return it soon."

"I can send it back with guards heading toward Keep Ross. It should not be more than a couple of days."

Robena didn't meet his gaze when he looked toward her. Instead, she went to sit in front of the hearth with Isla.

"I will miss our walks," Robena said, meaning it.

"I wish ye would stay," Isla remarked. "It is nice to have a friend."

"Once the bairn is born, ye must come to the village. I will do my best to come and visit as well." Robena informed Isla, who smiled warmly. "Admittedly, it will not be the same."

They remained in companionable silence, Robena not wishing to move, as the uncertainty of her future waited. Whether to remain in the cottage and seek employment at the house, or move on, either way, she would be alone and without Finn.

"I will ensure Bryce brings me to visit often. It is not as if he does much," Isla remarked, and both laughed softly so not to be heard. Robena had no doubt that Isla would keep her husband in check and slowly guide him to maturing.

CHAPTER TWELVE

WHEN ROSS GUARDS arrived the next morning, it did not surprise Artair. Darach knew he was there and had instructed them to stop and inform him of what happened.

He found Torac and Erik waiting for him in the front parlor. Both had the flat expressions of men used to keeping emotions hidden.

"Ensure the men eat before we leave," Artair said, knowing the men must have left the keep while it was still dark.

"Yer mother has already seen to it. There are only ten of us and everyone is eating either in the dining room or in the kitchen," Erik informed him.

Torac met his gaze. "Our laird received a report of a group of six men coming to the village for food and other things. No one recognized them. Two had bandages, making it suspicious."

Erik let out a breath. "Guards from the southern post went in search but did not find them. They did come across an abandoned campsite. They believe the men either left the Isle or headed north. Either way, it seems they are gone from the southern shore."

He continued. "We have trackers and archers with us. We can track them if they went north."

"I agree with it," Artair said. "What does Darach wish me

to do?"

"Ye are to remain at the southern post. Divide the men and assign areas to patrol. He also wishes for ye to meet with the villagers and ensure the people are well taken care of. Since the current constable needs to be relieved of his duties, a new one must be appointed."

Artair was glad for the orders. It gave him a plan of action for the months ahead. He would also be able to visit his parents regularly and perhaps start building his own home. Perhaps instead of building on the family lands, he could ask Darach to allow him to build closer to Taernsby. Not only would it be more beneficial, but it would also be a place he could come to time and again between different assignments.

"I will ensure all is prepared for us to depart shortly," Artair said, deciding it was time to go in search of Robena.

"Ah, there ye are, son," His father entered the parlor. "I was just speaking with the guards. It sounds as if the last of the evildoers have fled. Well done."

Although he could not take credit for it, his father's words were encouraging. "Aye, it is good news."

"If I could have a word with ye." His father beckoned toward the study. They walked side-by-side down the corridor.

Just then Robena walked by with her bundle of clothes in a sack. A maid hurried toward her and they spoke. She pulled her shawl over her shoulders and followed the maid toward the kitchen.

She would see Torac there. Immediately, Artair wanted to spin around.

"I wonder how long it will be before ye admit to yerself to be enamored of the lass," his father mused. "Probably not until it is too late."

"Too late?" Artair replied absent mindedly. "What do ye mean?"

"After she goes away . . . or marries another." His father ushered him into his study. "Let us speak about yer plans."

They settled into two chairs and Artair studied his father. Thankfully, Angus' coloring was good, his mind and eyesight remained keen.

"Ye have informed me multiple times of not having any wish to settle. Is that still the case?"

For some reason the statement sounded stark and, in a way, empty. Did he plan to live a nomad's life for the rest of his existence? Would he continue on quest after quest until too old to do so?

And yet, he had made the pronouncement time and again to never settle, never remain in one place for too long, and definitely never marry.

"Aye I do not plan to settle. Not for many years, until forced to."

"Son, I am going to ask that ye allow me time to work with Bryce to get him to become more responsible and learn to run the estate. I grow old and despite my recovery, I have to face the fact that I require help. Although I recovered from the last bout of whatever that was, I am tired most times."

There was warmth in his father's eyes and Artair realized he'd been acting strong for them. In the depths of the hazel gaze there was a silent request for him not to make things harder by asking questions or denying the inevitable.

Perhaps it would be a few months or even a pair of years before his father left them. It was, however, imperative Bryce learn as much as possible and take over the responsibilities of being a landowner.

Artair finally nodded. "I agree to not intercede and when I do visit to remain neutral and do my best to help, not hinder the process of Bryce's learning."

His father stood. "I must ride out to see about the farmers. I will not see ye off."

As they were about to walk out, his father placed a hand on Artair's shoulder. "I do not know what it is ye seek, but I hope ye find it."

Unable to keep from it, Artair threw his arms around his father and hugged him close. "Thank ye for being an understanding father."

He was clearing his throat as he entered the front parlor and spotted Bryce. His brother seemed in good spirits. "Ye leave today I hear?"

It was hard to bite back the sarcastic remark that Bryce no doubt expected. Instead, Artair nodded. "Aye. I am about to seek Robena and ensure the cart is prepared for us."

"I just saw her outside. She is speaking to one of the guards. I will say, brother, if ye are not interested in the lass, that man certainly is."

Letting out a slow breath, Artair met Bryce's gaze. "Go with father today and keep an eye on him. Do not allow him to go alone any longer."

At once Bryce's expression changed to one of worry. "Did something happen? He seems better of late."

Artair shook his head. "He puts up a brave front, for us, for mother. Send a messenger to the south post if ye require me to return for anything."

His brother nodded. "I will."

In that moment, Artair realized that given a task involving their father, Bryce took it seriously, and some of the worry about his brother not following through on taking on more responsibility lessened.

"I appreciate what ye do for them," Artair said. "Can I ask ye something?"

When Bryce nodded, Artair met his gaze. "If I had remained here and not gone to work for Darach, would ye have done something different with yer life?"

His brother was silent for a moment, his gaze on the floor. "I always hoped to go away to study literature. Edinburgh or Glasgow perhaps."

He shrugged. "I acquired books and taught myself what I could. Some days, I am not sure if I would have actually gone. At times I think aye, I would have and not returned for years. Other times, I cannot abide the thought of being far from home."

"If ye ever need to go, require time away to do something, I will support ye in it," Artair said, meaning it.

Bryce's face brightened. "I will give it some thought. Of course, now I must see about Isla and the bairn. Perhaps in the future I would like that very much."

After biding his mother farewell, Artair went to the kitchen to pick up a basket of food the housekeeper had prepared.

It surprised him that Robena was sitting at the table and not still outside with Torac.

She turned to him as he bid the cook farewell.

Artair did not feel compelled to speak to her. For some reason resentment stopped him from saying anything. There was a chance what he would say would come across as jealousy or even anger at her seeming to like Torac's attentions.

It was doubtful she had any intentions when it came to men. As a matter of fact, he got the impression her mind was on finding work and waiting for her son's return.

"Let us go, Robena." He kept his tone even.

They settled on the bench in the cart. Four guards including Erik were to escort them, while the other six, which included Torac, had gone on ahead.

As they began, Artair had to hold back his formidable horse as the beast seemed to consider being hitched to a wagon an insult and tried to gallop.

"I do not think Hagar is happy," Artair muttered. "I may have to ride him and ask one of the guards to hitch their horse if he continues to be unmanageable." He looked around to the other horses, all bred for war, and realized none of them would be any meeker than his.

Robena frowned. "I apologize. Perhaps I should have not asked for a cart."

"It is done now. Hagar will have to do as ordered."

"I must return the coins ye gave me. It is too much. I know it is yer money."

Several days earlier he'd acquired a new pouch from his father and taken money from his coffer to replenish it. The amount he'd given Robena was not large, but more than she would probably make by working as a servant for a pair of years.

"No, I insist ye keep it. Ye do not have a husband to support ye, and this way ye can take yer time about deciding what to do."

"Ye have done too much for me already. I am not sure how I feel about it. I will accept it if ye ask Alpena if I can help at the guard post. I can cook and clean."

Immediately Artair considered that Torac would be there when not patrolling.

He looked to Erik. "What are your orders?"

"To track and ensure all the intruders have indeed left." The blond man huffed as he considered. "I will first spend a pair of days searching the local area. Then we leave."

"Who do ye take with ye?"

"The four that rode ahead, and I will ask Struan if he wishes to go. He is one of the best at tracking. Will ye come with us?"

Erik had good plans. Artair and Stuart had often been called to do tracking and he itched to go. However, with Darach's orders, he had work to complete in the village.

"I must see about order in the village as ye informed me. Although I do enjoy tracking, I suppose this time I will be unable to assist."

As they continued, Artair spoke again to Robena. "If someone is not present to ensure yer well-being, being around so many men may prove . . . uncomfortable. Other than Alpena and the two helpers who are older, married women, we try to keep young women away. It is up to ye however, if ye think to be able to handle it."

Despite the warmer weather, Robena kept her shawl tight around her shoulders. It was as if she was protecting herself or perhaps closing herself off from him.

The companionable silence didn't bother Artair. He needed time to think and consider his father's words. Everyone acted as if they knew what he should do. It was as if his choice to not settle or never marry was the wrong one in everyone else's opinions.

There was more to life than to be tied down in one place. The resistance to it was not new. Besides, it wasn't as if he could not devote himself to one woman. He could. However, it was unlikely that he would ever find a woman who would agree to his unwillingness to be present, or to marry.

Additionally, he wasn't sure what would happen in his long absences. Surely whoever he decided to partner with would become lonely and seek solace in another's arms.

He slid a look to Robena, who studied the passing scenery. She was a beautiful woman. The only reason she was not with someone was probably out of respect for her time of mourning. Despite her quiet nature, she was strong-willed and stood her ground.

They had made love. Artair could not remember the last time he'd felt so lost in a woman. Admittedly, he rarely sought out a woman for sex, and when he'd done so in the past, it had been mostly a purely physical experience, nothing memorable. With Robena, the sensations and emotions were so raw that just thinking about it made it hard not to imagine being with her again.

She appealed to every part of him. His mind, body, and, if he wasn't careful, his heart.

Clearing his throat, he turned his mind away and thought of the situation with his family. Hopefully Bryce would step up and do what was required of him. His father needed the help and had much to teach his brother.

"It seems my cottage remains standing." Robena interrupted his thoughts and he realized they were nearly upon the village.

He turned to Erik. "Go ahead to the southern post. I will deposit Miss Robena and be there shortly."

The men galloped ahead to a road leading toward the sea, while he turned the wagon to the right down another, less-used path.

"I can take ye into the village to purchase any needed supplies. Ye will require food and such."

Robena glanced over her shoulder to the back of the wagon. "The cook allowed me to pick items from the kitchen and garden, and I have bread and herbs to boil for tea. I will go in a pair of days."

"Are ye dreading being alone?" Artair wasn't sure why he asked. Of course, she could not be happy about the situation. "I mean, I know ye will be sad. However, perhaps ye can have a friend come and stay."

"There is no need for company. I need time alone." She sighed. "Ye have been more than kind."

When they pulled up to the cottage, Artair climbed down and motioned for her to remain. "Let me make sure no one is about."

He walked to the door and entered. It seemed all was as Robena had left it. Nonetheless, he hurried up the steps to the bedrooms and looked around. Beyond a door was a small cot with Finn's belongings. Artair hesitated, taking in the tidy space.

When he turned, Robena was behind him, her gaze past him to the room. Covering her face with both hands, she began to sob, gut wrenching cries coming from a pain so deep it was palpable.

Artair took her in his arms and did his best to soothe her despite knowing nothing would. She would eventually stop crying, but her heart would remain broken.

"My boy," she cried out between sobs. "My sweet boy." Her body shook as the pain racked her.

He'd never witnessed such raw emotion, even in the battlefield. Comrades grieving the lost had been an expected reaction. This was a mother mourning the loss of a child torn from her in an unfair way, her cries tore through him.

Leading her to the other bedroom, he sat and pulled her onto his lap. Robena looked up, her face wet with tears, and took a deep shaky breath. "I do not know if I can withstand this. It hurts so very much."

She stood and raced from the room.

There was a crashing sound and Artair hurried to see what she'd done. She stood in Finn's room, throwing things about, screaming and wailing as items flew through the air and crashed against the walls, some breaking into pieces. He waited outside, somehow knowing she needed to allow her grief free reign.

It was a while later her cries softened. He went inside and found her on the floor clutching one of her son's tunics against her chest.

Sliding his arms beneath her, he lifted her and carried her back to her bedroom and placed her upon the bed. "I will boil ye some of those herbs the cook sent for ye."

She didn't reply but laid upon the bed, a blank expression on her face.

Back downstairs, Artair unloaded the few things from the

wagon. Then he unhitched Hagar, who lifted his huge hooves from the ground and shook his great mane to ensure Artair once again was aware of his annoyance of being hindered in such a humiliating way for a warhorse.

Artair guided him to a corral and placed feed for him in a stone trough, then drew water from the well and filled a small vessel for the horse to drink from.

Taking another bucket of water into the house, he went about getting a fire started in the hearth and boiling the herbs for Robena to drink.

He suspected his mother had instructed the cook to give Robena the proper herbs as they no doubt expected her reaction upon returning.

A soft smile curved his lips. Women were such clever creatures. Men were reactive and went on instinct. But women, they were the ones with the notions that made everything better. Although delicate in some ways, of the two, male and female, in his opinion, women were the stronger.

CHAPTER THIRTEEN

ROBENA WOKE WITH a slight headache. Beside her Artair slept, his breathing soothing to her raw senses.

Shivering, she moved closer to him, snuggling against his back, allowing the warmth of his body to seep into hers. A coldness had taken over her and despite the thick bedding she could not get warm. Sometime during the night, Artair must have come to the bed and lay down next to her, but atop the blankets, with a separate cover of his own. His thick tartan.

Such was it between them, everything felt so natural, that him in her bed did not feel strange in the least. It was dangerous, that they could be so compatible, but at the same time the truth was clear; that Artair did not plan to ever settle and in time he would leave.

Today she would speak to him and ask that he not seek her anymore. His going would be another wound to her already shredded heart, but she was falling in love with him and the longer they were together, the harder it would be to let him go.

A soft snore sounded, and she smiled. He was such a kind and caring man. It was the first time she'd met a man who did everything he could to ensure she was well.

It was reassuring that for the time being Artair would be near. He'd informed her of the laird's orders to oversee the village. However, she had no doubt that as soon as matters settled, he would leave to seek a new adventure.

Closing her eyes, she prayed to sleep a while longer. She didn't want this moment to end.

She must have fallen asleep, because when Artair jostled her, Robena yawned widely. He'd rolled to his back and slipped an arm under her head, so she was cradled in the crook of it, her head on his shoulder.

"How do ye feel?" he asked, his voice groggy.

"I do not know."

"I haven't slept this late in a long time. Tired."

She let out a breath. "Me either. Ye should go. I am sure ye have much to do."

For a long moment, Artair didn't reply. "I will return and ensure ye are well."

Words stuck in her throat, and she fought not to begin crying again. As it was, her eyes felt dry and swollen from the night before.

"It feels so natural to be speaking to ye, here in my bed," Robena said with a soft chuckle. "Although it is most unusual, and we should not be here together. If a villager were to happen by and see yer horse . . ." She left the rest unsaid.

When he pressed a kiss to her temple, she sighed at the sweetness of it.

"Artair. I must ask that ye stay away from me. It is best that we do not spend time together any longer."

He gave her an incredulous look. "Why?"

After pressing a kiss to his cheek, she slid from the bed and wrapped in a long robe. "My heart cannot withstand any more pain and the more we are together, the more I wish for ye to remain."

She took a long breath. "And because I know ye do not plan to ever settle and ye have many responsibilities which do not include me. I can take care of myself and need to learn to be independent." Robena bit her bottom lip to keep from crying. Her emotions raw and exposed.

When he sat up and remained on her bed, she couldn't help but wish things were different and the vision before her, a handsome man with hair mused from sleep upon her bed was hers to keep. Not just any man, but him, who she felt so at ease with. Just a lift of his brow made her body tremble with want.

"Ye should not be alone. Will ye promise me to spend time with someone from the village? A friend?"

"I will visit Heather; she always needs help with her bairns. It will be a welcome distraction."

When he stood and neared, she froze, willing him to walk past and not touch her. But he did. He cupped her face and lifted it up so that he could peer into her eyes. "Ye are a special woman Robena. If things were different . . ."

"Do not say it. It matters not what would happen *if*," Robena said staring deep into his eyes. "Ye are not willing to give yerself to me and that is what is."

Closing his eyes as if in pain, he lowered his forehead to hers. "I will keep an eye on ye. Seek me if ye require anything." With that he turned and walked out of the room.

Robena waited, not wanting to go downstairs until he was gone. It would be a few moments before he would finish putting on his boots and strap the scabbard to his back.

Tears spilled down her cheeks. She dreaded facing the day alone. The two people she cared for the most were soon to be gone from her life.

It was a while later that she heard the cart and horse depart. She went to the window to watch him ride away. He looked back at the cottage several times, as if considering returning. When she turned from the window, she noted his tartan remained on the bed.

She would pay a village boy to return it so Artair would not use the item as an excuse to come back.

Later that day, she sat downstairs in front of the hearth, wrapped in Artair's tartan. She drank some of the herbal tea and allowed herself to rest. She'd eaten a small meal earlier and inspected the pens that her father had built. The following day, she would go to the village and, with the money Artair had given her, she'd purchase a pair of goats and some chickens. It would give her the ability to begin her life without need of others.

The older couple she helped with gardening would assist in getting the animals to the cottage, since she planned to buy from them. The only thing left to decide was how to make a living.

Robena studied her surroundings. There was little she needed. Thankfully her parents had kept the cottage repaired and ensured to have sturdy well-made furniture. The only thing she had to worry about was clothing and food.

When her gaze went to the top of the stairs, her heart squeezed. Finn was well taken care of, and she was sure he was happy. It was his environment after all. He'd spent many months with the Mackay clan. Did he miss her at all?

As tears spilled down her face, she burrowed into the tartan, her sobs muffled by the thick wool cloth.

THE VILLAGE WAS busier than usual. The warmer weather as late spring set in meant traveling merchants visited the square bringing new items to be fought over.

Upon seeing her, Heather waved Robena closer to her stall where she was selling eggs and chickens. Robena allowed the woman to hug her as she fought not to cry anew. "I heard and I am so very sorry about Finn. I am sure he will return soon."

"I hope so." Robena turned to pat her friend's children's heads and then inspected the eggs and chicks. "I will purchase eggs and a pair of chickens from ye."

Heather beamed, "They're good laying hens. I will gift them to ye. No one has offered to buy them."

"I would like to help ye in some way as payment."

"Will ye mind my stall?" Heather asked. "I am dying to see what the peddler has."

Moments later, Robena sat with a bairn on her lap and two at her feet sleeping soundly atop folded blankets their mother had placed for them under the table.

In the distance, several horsemen appeared, and she immediately recognized Artair. Her heart skipped a beat and her stomach tightened at the sight of him. His light brown hair glistened in the sunlight and atop the huge warhorse, he appeared formidable. The men rode toward the constable's house, and she was glad to be able to avoid him.

"Lad," she said turning to Heather's eldest boy who played nearby. "Take this tartan to the constable's house. Ask for a man named Artair and give it to him."

The boy grinned widely at being given such an important task. With the tartan in hand, he raced away.

Heather returned a few moments later, a content smile on

her face. "It is nice to move around without bairns hanging from me."

Despite the sadness in her heart, Robena smiled. "I do not mind helping ye."

Heather's expression brightened. "If ye would work my stall a few days, I will pay ye from the sales. It would free me up to do more at home. The garden is in dire need of tending and I am always behind in my chores."

"I agree," Robena said. "I need something to do, and this is perfect." She let out a sigh of relief. It would not be much, but enough that she could save and be able to pay for any needs that happened. Along with the money she had left after buying the goats, she would not want for much.

Heather's eldest boy rushed back; his face flushed from the exercise and no longer carrying the tartan.

"So ye found him then?" Robena asked, looking in the direction of the constable's house.

The boy nodded. "He said to thank ye."

Her friend gave her a questioning look. "Whose tartan did ye have?"

"Artair Ross, the laird's cousin. He allowed me to use it yesterday." Robena met her friend's gaze and Heather nodded, understanding what needed to be said should not be done so in public.

When additional Ross guards arrived at the village square, she noted Torac was one of them. He acknowledged her with a nod but did not move near to speak to her. Robena wondered if he was aware that Artair had not come to the post all night.

Torac was a handsome man and had shown kindness and interest in her. It was obvious he wanted more than friendship.

However, the timing was not good. At the moment, her heart was too overwrought to consider anyone other than Artair.

"He's a handsome one," Heather teased. "Ye know 'im?"

"I do. He is kind."

Heather gave her a knowing look. "Once ye are ready, ye will not have any problem finding a good husband. If ye wish for one."

"I do not know anything right now," Robena replied with honesty. "Sometimes I just wish to hide in my cottage and never leave."

It was nice to have someone to confide in, although she mused that Heather could not relate. Her parents were alive, she had a loving husband and healthy children. It was Heather's choice to set up the stall. Her husband did not make her do it.

"I have not seen yer parents in a while," Robena remarked. "Are they well?"

"They are well, still in the tiny cottage next to ours. Mother is keeping the youngest," Heather said with a chuckle. "She refuses to watch these two, says they are too unruly." She looked to her slumbering children with a soft smile. "Look like angels right now. But when they wake they can be the opposite." Her friend chuckled.

For a while longer, Robena remained with Heather, then went to the older couple's home.

The sun was setting by the time Robena arrived home with her new acquisitions of two goats and the chickens.

Robena had grown up helping her parents tend to the animals but needing to be sure to keep the animals in her care healthy she'd asked the old man a great deal.

Settling for the night, she brought water from the well and filled her small wooden tub with heated water. Once she rested and spent a few days at the cottage, she would decide what days to help Heather and then spend other days tending to her animals and starting a garden.

Life would be different, but it would be as she wished it to be.

IT TOOK A long while before the constable was sober enough to answer questions in a way that made sense. The man's bloodshot eyes moved from the floor to the side, never meeting Artair's.

"I am not perfect, but I care about the villagers. Ye cannot say I 'aven't done me job," he insisted.

Artair slammed his fist onto the table, making the man jump. "I have yet to see ye help with the fight against the attacks. Did ye ever go see about the wounded?"

The man held his head. "I am sick. Cannot help that I am not well."

"What ye are is a drunk," Struan interjected. "Ye smell like sour ale."

The constable narrowed his eyes. "If ye want to take me job, ye will have to go to the Laird."

It was hard not to take the man by the neck and shake him. "I am Artair Ross, the laird's cousin, am here on his behalf to remove ye."

A woman bustled into the room with a pitcher and cups. "I brought some mead for ye." She looked to them; worry etched on her craggy face. “We have nowhere to go. Surely my laird is not so cruel to kick us out into the cold.”

“It is spring,” Struan replied, annoyed. “With the deaths from the attacks there are several empty homes. Ye can both crawl into one of them and quickly turn it into a smelly hovel.”

Artair pressed his lips together to keep from laughing at Struan’s rude remark. Obviously, neither the constable or his wife cared much for bathing or cleaning from the way the house smelled.

“Be out by tomorrow,” Artair told the man who laid his head on folded arms atop the table. “No excuses. Otherwise, my men will come and drag ye out.”

Artair looked to a young guard. “The house will have to be cleaned thoroughly before anyone can live there. Find a pair of women in the village who will do it for coin.”

He placed a young guard at the front door when they walked out. “See about a cat or two. I saw wee mice about.”

Struan shook his head. “I have half a mind to drag them out now and throw them into the sea.”

Before mounting, Artair stuffed his tartan into the bag hanging from the saddle. The fragrance that wafted from it not only soothed his nose from the smells of the house they’d just walked from, but also immediately reminded him of Robena.

Obviously, she’d sent the tartan so he did not have an excuse to return to see her.

“Who do ye think should fill the position of constable?” he asked Struan. The warrior had been assigned to the southern post often over the years and knew most of the villagers well. From what Artair could tell, the people seemed to know and like him.

Struan shrugged. "There are a few who would not mind doing it. I am wondering however, if any of them would do a good job."

As Struan listed several men and explained their experience and qualities, Artair listened and tried to picture such a person representing the laird to the people.

"Why have the villagers not come to see Darach about this man?" he asked.

"Because the late laird heard their complaints and did nothing for it." Struan said. "Apparently, he even threw one of them into the dungeon for complaining."

His late uncle had been an excessively cruel man. Artair had not gotten to know him well, as he'd done his best to avoid the man while serving in the guard ranks. Everyone in Clan Ross knew how horrible their laird was.

Keeping mostly to inside the home or traveling meant the late laird had little to do with the guardsmen.

"We should head back to the guard house," Artair told his companions. As they rode past the village, Erik and Torac appeared ahead. Upon seeing them, the duo slowed.

"I thought ye were to head north to track the men," Artair said. "What happened?"

"They were seen leaving on bìrlinns. We spoke to several fishermen and it seems that the bunch had decided to leave. They had the injured with them."

They rode in silence until arriving at the building and once the horses were seen to, went inside to eat.

The meal was flavorful, but Artair could not enjoy it. All day he'd had an uneasy feeling that he could not get rid of. Something in the air was not quite right and it annoyed him that he could not put his finger on it.

He strolled into the kitchen, unable to be still. "Did ye need something Mister Artair?" Alpena asked, surprised at his appearance. "How is the young lass doing?"

"Seems well. I saw her from afar, she was tending to a stall." He lowered to a chair at the table where Alpena ate.

"In my opinion women have a sense of things that is stronger than men," Artair stated.

Alpena continued eating, glancing to him for only a moment. "What bothers ye?"

"I do not know," Artair said. "A feeling I cannot rid myself of. Something bad about to happen."

"All is well with yer family?"

"I just left them two days ago. All was well."

"What about the attackers?" Alpena sat back and looked at him. "Any threats?"

"They've gone and no threats I am aware of."

She considered him for a moment. "Mayhap ye are just worried."

"It could be," Artair said pushing back. "I think ye are right."

Alpena's next statement however stopped him in his tracks. "If it is a strong sense, then ye should pay heed. It could be a warning that ye should prepare for whatever will come."

Instead of going to his tiny bed chamber, he walked outside and looked up to the sky. It was not a starry night. There was a slight haze that made it hard to see more than a patch of sky here and there.

The pounding of horse's hooves got his attention, and he ran toward the front of the building. A man dismounted and hurried to the door, banging on the stout panels.

"What is it?" Artair called out.

The man whirled around just as the door opened and guards came running from the other side of the building.

"A ship has capsized or sunk offshore. There are bodies and items washing up now."

Within moments most of the guardsmen were mounted and raced toward where the man had instructed. It was easy to find the area of the shipwreck by the many torches lighting the night.

The guards worked with fishermen in boats going out in hopes of saving people. There were screams of excitement from people who found survivors, and at other times exclamations of sadness.

Artair hurried along the shore pulling people from the water, most of them dead. There had to have been many passengers on the ship, because by his count there were ten bodies already and four survivors.

Boats headed back toward shore, and he assumed they'd also found more people.

"Artair!" A call came from atop the embankment. A man waved his arms. "Artair!"

"What now?" he muttered making his way up to where the man stood. He recognized the young man who worked at the stables at his father's house. His stomach sank.

"What is it Jacob?"

"There is a missive for ye," the young man said, coming closer. He held the reins to his horse and since there was nowhere to tie it, he'd not felt comfortable leaving it.

"Who sends this?" Artair asked, squinting at the parchment in the dark. "I cannot see anything."

"From yer father," Jacob replied.

Artair looked around and upon spying a woman walking past with a torch, he called her over. She stood impatiently by as he read the message.

Son,

Yer brother has died. He fell from his horse and hit his head. We had to bury him straight away. Ye should consider coming home.

Yer father, AR

His father had initialed it, the familiar, strongly printed letters that ended all his correspondence.

It was as if the air was torn from his body and it was hard to see. His chest constricted, making it impossible to speak. All he could do was stare at the messenger, who seemed to understand his reaction.

"Yer father has asked that I remain and accompany ye back."

Silently, Artair looked over his shoulder at the ongoing activities. "We go at first light. Go to the guard post, just over there." Artair motioned in the direction he'd come from. "Ask for Alpena, she will feed ye and see about finding ye a place to rest."

The young man left and Artair stood for a long moment rereading the short message. How could it be? Bryce was gone. Was his impetuous, willful brother truly dead?

Feeling as if a boulder rested on his shoulders, Artair trudged back to the shoreline just as two boats came ashore with people who had been pulled from the water.

Survivors screamed and cried, begging the men to return to the water and search for loved ones. Many of the fishermen accompanied by guards continued the search, but as time passed, the prospects of finding survivors were in all probability gone.

It was a horrible scene as several more bodies joined the ones found earlier and all types of items washed ashore. Some villagers raced to and from the water fishing out items they'd either keep or try to sell later. It was customary, but sad as the survivors were too fraught with despair to look for any belongings.

By the time the sun rose, those who remained ambled about in a daze. A few fishermen volunteered to go back out and search for survivors who had perhaps clung to life through the night. Most of the guards had spent the night transporting people to the village church and the dead to a barn behind it.

Some remained with the people, doing what could be done, while others came to the shoreline, driven by curiosity and the idea of what happened.

A man who'd seemed to have survived the ordeal without trauma explained to Artair that the ship had been caught in a storm and sustained so much damage they'd floated for several days without a mast. Then the worst happened, they'd hit rocks, splitting the bottom of the ship.

Even as the ship sank, the survivors had managed to hold on until the very end. There had been two small rowboats hanging from the sides, but they'd quickly filled, and the people had rowed away to another shore.

The morning sun brought with it a scene of items strewn

on the shore below. Artair had managed a few moments of sleep on a bench outside the village church. He'd been too exhausted to walk to the post to find his own bed.

Struan lowered to sit next to him and yawned widely. "Go to yer family, Artair. Erik and I will take care of the people until ye return."

It was as if an ax had been driven into the center of his chest, the pain so raw and real, he flinched. There was no avoiding facing the fact his brother was dead. Artair looked away from Struan and let out a breath. "I will return as soon as possible."

His gaze moved to the shoreline. "Dispatch a messenger to inform Darach of what has happened. Speak to the survivors and find where they wish to go. I am confident our laird will assist them in their continued travel."

After a quick meal and washing up, Artair and the young man from his father's house mounted and prepared to leave.

He gave further instructions, insisting that the guards ensure every survivor was properly fed and had a place to sleep.

Alpena rushed to him. "Do not worry. The women from the village are gathering to cook and collect what is needed."

When passing where Robena lived on the outskirts of town, Artair took one last look over his shoulder toward the small cottage.

Because of his brother's death, his choices were gone, and it meant he would never be able to be with Robena again. There was no doubt in his mind that with Bryce gone, Isla's parents would demand that Artair marry her to keep the bairn from being born fatherless.

They had every right, and it would be insulting to her family and his for Artair not to do it.

The young man looked to him. "I must stop for a moment."

"Who is yer family?" Artair asked, for some reason needing to know more about the young man who'd worked for his family since a very young lad.

"My father is named like me, Jacob McGill," he replied. "He works in the village as the baker."

Artair nodded, recalling the jolly baker who always seemed to be in good spirits. "Yer father seems a kind man. Do ye have siblings?"

"Aye, two brothers and one sister." Jacob studied him for a moment. "I am very sorry about yer brother."

Bringing the horses to a stop, both dismounted. Artair remained with the horses while Jacob relieved himself and then they switched.

"Do ye know if my brother and Isla married before . . .?"

Jacob shook his head. "I do not think so."

UPON ARRIVING AT his family home, things were as he expected. The house was draped in mourning. His ashen-faced father greeted him, with eyes misting as he met Artair's gaze.

"He's gone, son. Yer brother is gone." Upon uttering the words, his father fell against him, sobs racking through his body. One thing was certain, Artair and his brother had never doubted how much their parents loved them. This demonstration of grief was not unexpected.

After finally composing himself, his father motioned toward a doorway. "Go greet yer mother."

In the sitting room, his mother rested with her head on a stack of pillows. She sat up and held out her arms. "Oh Artair, if only ye had been here, it might not have happened."

It wasn't time to ask questions. Instead, for the second time in as many days, he held a grieving mother.

"Where is Isla?" He asked his father who looked on.

"Upstairs. She has been in her bedchamber since it happened."

Bettina walked in and helped Iona to stand. "Let us take ye to have a warm bath and a bit of a sleep," the woman said soothingly.

"I will be up to sit with ye once ye are settled," Artair reassured her.

His father walked in and sat. "We had to bury him right away. I and a several local men searched for a pair of days. Wild beasts found him before we did."

"I hope he was dead before," Artair said, his throat constricted at the thought of his brother laying out in pain and alone.

His father nodded and wiped clumsily at tears. "I am sure he was. The back of his head was bashed in badly. The horse must have been scared and threw him."

While his father talked, Artair poured two glasses of whisky. They drank in silence, each considering a future without Bryce.

IT WAS A week later that he returned to the seaside village. Everything had changed. His life altered forever.

He and his father agreed Artair should finish his duties at the southern post before returning to live there at his family lands.

As if a massive boulder rested on his shoulders, he fought to sit upright in the saddle. When the village came into view, he let out a sigh of relief, exhaustion from the days prior finally consuming him.

In the days after arriving home, he'd ridden daily with his father to meet the farmers and others who depended on the family. Each day accepting condolences and doing his best not to break down at witnessing his parents' and Isla's grief.

He and Isla were married one rainy afternoon, the weather outside as dreary as the ceremony itself. After, she'd refused to spend any time in his company, instead recusing herself, only leaving the bedchamber to eat at last meal.

How she acted was understandable for someone who planned to marry for love, only to end up with a husband whom she had no desire to be with.

When he'd told her his plans to leave and go to the southern post, her relief was palpable. Artair did not take it personally.

Now he had to serve as constable and ensure the village was in good hands before leaving, never to return.

CHAPTER FOURTEEN

ROBENA STOOD OUTSIDE a small cottage where three women who'd survived the shipwreck were to live. She, along with other women of the village, had filled their cupboards and ensured they had what was needed.

For different reasons, the trio had asked to remain there and not travel further on the bìrlinns provided by the laird. Most of the survivors had continued their treks to mainland Scotland or to their families.

Two of the women who'd remained had been widowed and buried their husbands there. The third had lost her entire family and did not have anywhere to go.

Once Robena's chores were done that day, her plan was to remain at home for several days and do absolutely the minimal required.

She'd not seen Artair in several days. The only person who'd been around helping and, on occasion sharing a meal with her, at the village square, was Torac. His quiet presence had been nice; however, she was fully aware she'd never be able to develop deep feelings for him.

Torac walked toward her, he'd offer to walk her home and she steeled herself. It was time to ensure she didn't mislead him. He was a good man.

"Robena," he began.

"I plan to visit my friend Heather and inform her of my plans to rest. She and I share duties of the stall at the village square as ye know." Robena could not stop talking, hoping he did not press the matter of accompanying her.

"I brought ye this," he held out a small bundle. The aroma wafting from it made her mouth water. "Tis a meat pie. Alpena makes the best."

She accepted it, smiling up at him. "Ye are too kind to me, Torac."

They walked in companionable silence in the direction of Heather's home. She wasn't sure what to say to him in parting.

"Anything new?" She asked, hoping he'd bring up his duty assignments so she could gauge how much longer he would be there.

"Aye, Artair returned. I think ye would like to know he is married now."

Her sharp intake of breath was audible and Robena was aware the reaction wounded Torac. He had romantic intentions toward her after all.

"I see it hurts ye. I should not have blurted it out," Torac said, his voice soft. "I apologize."

Robena turned and placed her hand on his forearm. "I needed to know. Thank ye for telling me." She tried her best to give him a reassuring look but wasn't sure if it came across. Then she rose to her toes and pressed a kiss to his jawline.

Taking the opportunity, he wrapped his arms around her, holding her close. "I do not like to see ye hurt. Artair is not worthy of yer love."

His words mortified her. Had it been so obvious to everyone that she was in love with Artair Ross?

"Who did he marry?"

"The woman who is to bear his brother's bairn."

"It is a noble thing to do," she replied, the burning in her stomach threatening to make her sick. "I best go. Thank ye for the pie."

Robena pushed out of his arms and hurried to Heather's house. Instead of entering, she rounded to the back of the cottage and threw up.

"Did ye eat something rotted?" Heather peered out the window.

"No," Robena replied straightening. "Just overly tired."

Thankfully, Heather did not ask any more questions. She was too busy with the children and preparing a meal to pay her much mind.

After visiting with her friend until feeling better, Robena hurried home grateful for the time alone that awaited.

Her cottage welcomed her with warmth and coziness. Robena set water to boil and left the front door and windows open to air it out a bit.

Just as she settled into a chair, footsteps sounded. One of her goats ambled in, as if it were the most natural thing in the world. It looked to her with unblinking eyes and then began to nibble one of the blankets she'd thrown over the back of a chair.

"No." Robena went to the naughty animal and tugged the blanket from its mouth. "If ye continue to escape the pen, ye will be gobbled up by a wild beast."

Not seeming to care what she said, or that she tried to pull it toward the door, the animal backed away and went to the table to sniff at the basket of fruit. Then it rose to its hind legs in an attempt to reach the offerings.

Robena could not help it and laughed. She grabbed a plump pear and used it to entice the goat to follow her back to the pen. Once there, she divided the fruit with his companion, who seemed glad to see her friend.

Lingering at the pen, she watched the goats for a long time, not wishing to be alone with her thoughts.

Artair is married. She would never be with him again.

She'd not asked if he'd remain at the village. Hopefully not. The last thing she wanted was to see him. It would be doubly painful.

TWO DAYS LATER, Robena stood at the stall at the village market. There were plenty of eggs to be sold and she was glad when Alpena came and bought every single one. The woman then handed her coins and a small fruit cake.

"It is beautiful weather. I wish winter would never come." The woman lamented. "It makes my bones ache."

Robena itched to ask about Artair, but instead, she asked about helping. It was on her mind that she still had to repay the money Artair had given her. "If ye have mending or other tasks that need to be done, I can come and collect the items. I feel indebted to ye and Mister Ross."

"Nonsense, lass. People do for others because it is the way it should be."

It was later in the day when she spotted Torac and several other guards. The men came to the village almost daily on patrols.

Rarely did anyone get away with anything with the Ross detachment assigned there. However, there were a time or two that they were called to break up fights or attempt to catch thieves who traveled through on their way to a different destination.

As expected, Torac and the other man came to her stall. Torac's familiar dark gaze met hers. "How fare ye?"

"I am well. Time alone at home was what I needed."

"There is to be a bonfire tomorrow night," the other guard said. "Perhaps ye could tell the women at the cottage?"

Her lips curved. It was obvious one must have caught the young man's eye.

"I certainly will. When I am done here, I plan to stop by their cottage today."

When the guard ambled away, Torac remained. "Will ye be attending?"

Truthfully, she'd not given it much thought. Bonfires were often to celebrate an occasion. In this case it was the celebration of the establishment of the village.

More times than not, it was best for women to attend in groups and be escorted by a male. Once men drank too much, it could make for chaos.

"I may go with the women."

"Good," he said smiling. "I will ensure to keep watch."

Over his shoulder she caught sight of a lone rider passing by. Instantly her stomach tumbled. It was Artair.

Thankfully, Torac didn't notice as he waited politely for a woman to make a purchase from Robena. While the woman sorted through the vegetables, Robena kept an eye on Artair, who rode up to the now empty constable's house and dismounted.

He didn't walk inside. Instead, he stood next to his horse and looked toward the village square. Robena prayed he'd not come closer.

Once the woman finished her purchase, Robena began to collect items, placing them in baskets to save for the next day.

"I am to take items to the women for them to cook. I will see ye tomorrow."

Torac studied her baskets. "Do ye require help?"

Robena explained she'd already hired a lad to assist. Just then, the lad she'd asked to help arrived.

Sending him off to take the caged hens to Heather's house, she lifted the basket of vegetables to take to the women's home.

THE FLAMES OF the bonfire danced merrily in the wind giving enough light for the groups gathered on blankets on the shore to see each other.

Fiddlers played lively tunes and people took turns dancing, clapping, and singing as the full moon rose over them. It was a beautiful night, but Robena couldn't help thinking of the one only a year earlier when she'd sat on the same blanket with Finn and one of the maids from the Mackay household.

They'd remained until late in the night, Finn finally succumbing to a deep sleep, his sweet face on her lap.

The flames bent sideways as a gust of wind came, a beautiful demonstration of two elements in a dance. It was mesmerizing to watch the display with the addition of the shadows of those dancing around the base.

Without her noticing until he arrive, Artair lowered himself to the blanket and sat next to her without speaking a word.

There was nothing to be said. That he was another woman's husband for the rest of their lives was not something that could be changed.

She understood he wanted to explain, to say something, but it didn't matter. He was never to be hers. Even before the death of his brother, he'd made it abundantly clear.

"I wish things were different," he finally said. "We could have enjoyed this night together."

Robena looked to the women next to her. None seemed to be paying any attention to her and Artair. Nonetheless, she didn't wish for them to overhear something that would later become ugly rumors.

Standing, she walked a few feet away and Artair followed.

"This night would not have been something we shared because ye did not wish for a relationship with me. Why would ye say that?"

His gaze, so familiar, met hers. "I wish I had married ye."

"Wishes will not change what is." Robena's heart ached at being unable to reach for him, to touch his face, to feel his kiss.

"Leave me be Artair. Nothing can be between us ever again. It hurts me to see ye right now."

For a long moment, he hesitated, then, to her surprise, leaned forward and pressed a kiss to her cheek, right beside her lips.

In the next instant, Artair was gone.

Several women screamed and Robena spun to see what happened. It took a minute to distinguished who fought, but the light from the bonfire gave her enough light and she gasped. Artair and Torac attacked each other like angry rams fighting for dominance.

Robena hurried back to the blanket, praying no one had noticed her speaking with Artair, hoping they wouldn't assume was her they fought over. She couldn't keep from looking on in astonishment as the grappling men rolled one across the rocky ground.

Men rushed to pull them apart, and it took all their strength to do so. Torac and Artair were so enraged that they managed to tear away from the men and clashed once more.

The next time they were pulled apart, their chests heaved, and blood dripped from broken noses and cut lips.

"That was something," one of the women said. "Which do ye prefer?" she asked Robena.

"Neither." She stood and hurried away, not wanting to be the cause of gossip.

It was probably too late.

The next day she would have to inform Torac she was not interested in any sort of relationship. It was best that he found a good woman who loved him unconditionally. She arrived at Heather's house and sat outside on a bench. After placing the blanket over her shoulders, she let out a breath. Why would Torac attack Artair? Had he mistaken Artair kissing her cheek for an unwanted advance?

Overhead a star fell across the sky and Robena tracked its path until it was no longer visible. If only Artair had stayed away. Everything he said was useless, if nothing else, his empty words made her chest ache in the strange echoing emptiness of unrequited love.

“There was a fight?” Heather said upon arriving. She carried a child, another whined softly while clutching her skirts.

“Stop crying Lizzie-Beth,” Heather cooed at the crying child. She then took the sleeping one and the crying one and sat them on the bench next to Robena. While Heather put the sleeping child to bed and warmed water, her husband arrived with the other two children. He gave her a tired smile and went inside.

Moments later the four children were rinsed of all sand and dirt, dressed in warm clothes and three sat on a bench inside drinking hot porridge. The youngest bairn slept soundly in its cradle.

“Thank you for helping,” Heather said with a smile. “Go to bed.”

Not long after, she settled to sleep, sharing a small room with two of the couple’s bairns.

Robena stared at the ceiling for a long time, replaying Artair’s words. Why had he told her his regrets? It mattered little now. Was he trying to make her feel better, or were those words spoken to soothe his own soul?

She lifted her hand to the place his lips had been. Once again, it was familiar. His closeness and presence reached into the depths of her being.

Turning to her side, she let out a breath and studied the moonlight streaming through the window.

THE NEXT DAY she was summoned by a lad who came to her at the stall at the market. There was little business that day as most slept in and rested from the night before.

“The constable wishes to see ye. ’E said it was important,”

the lad told her, his chest puffed out at being given such a responsibility.

Robena could not believe Artair would dare call her. Without a choice, she gave the lad a coin and asked him to mind the stand while she was gone. In all probability, he'd pocket the money for any sales, but she would be sure to hold him responsible if he did.

Upon entering the house where the constable lived and where villagers who needed resolutions went to seek help, Robena was struck by how well furnished and clean it now was.

Artair was in the front room, his back to her, looking out a large window to the sea.

"Why have ye called me?" Robena asked without preamble. "We cannot continue speaking."

He turned around and she could not keep her eyes from widening.

One eye was almost swollen shut, the corner of his lips was swollen and there were purple lumps on his temple and jaw.

"I wish to apologize and inform ye I will never seek ye out again. But that is not the only reason I summoned ye."

Robena crossed her arms and waited silently.

Artair cleared his throat. "There is the matter of the Mackay house. It seems yer late husband wished to ensure yer well-being. Ye are entitled to a portion of the sales."

He motioned to a pouch next to a ledger. "Sign it and take the money."

The large sum of money meant she could go away. Start a new life, perhaps somewhere in Scourie, and seek out Finn. Her hand trembled as she reached for it.

"I insist ye take out what ye gave me. I want to repay ye. I do not wish to beholden to anyone." She held it out toward him.

Nodding, he took the purse and pulled the top open. He counted out the money then pulled the strings closed again.

Robena met his gaze for a long time. "I wish ye happiness, Artair."

When he closed his eyes, she took the pouch and left.

CHAPTER FIFTEEN

Two months later.

WAILS EMANATING FROM behind the closed door announced the birth of Isla and Bryce's child.

Artair had been pacing the hallway, while his father sat in a chair with seeming calmness. When the sounds came, he jumped to his feet and they embraced.

"Praise be. The child sounds healthy," Angus Ross announced.

One of the maids hurried from the room and then returned with another in tow, carrying a pot of boiled water and more cloths.

"What happens?" Artair asked but was met with a slam of the door.

Finally, what seemed like hours later, his mother emerged. "It is a boy."

"How is Isla?" Artair asked.

"I am not sure," his mother replied with a shake of her head. "She is very pale and refusing to hold the bairn. It is as if she has no will to live."

"I will speak to her," Artair said, and his mother motioned to the doorway.

The room was bright with sunlight and candles. The smell of blood lingered in the air and he was shocked at how pale

Isla was. She followed his progress, seeming to urge him close.

"Ye must fight to recover fully. The bairn will need ye."

"Thank ye for what ye did. To marry me. I know ye love another and ye sacrificed yerself for my son." She did not reply to his statement, seeming to think it was not important.

Instead, she continued speaking, her gaze locked to him. "I must ask that ye bring him up as a proper Ross. To be noble, strong, and brave. To learn to be selfless and to remember me always."

Artair took her head. "Do not say these things. Ye will be here to see him grow up and become a man. Ye will take part in molding him."

Her hollow gaze met his. "We will see. I do not feel as if I will."

Artair didn't believe her. She was still grieving Bryce's death. Giving birth was an emotional experience and she was overwrought.

Going to the door, he motioned a maid closer. "Has the healer been sent for?"

"Aye," the maid said. "We hope she will arrive soon."

Turning back to the bed, he sat down and spent the rest of the day with Isla. She ate very little and when the bundled newborn was brought to her, she insisted Artair hold him.

"Ye must nurse him Isla," his mother insisted.

Finally, after much prodding, the bairn was attached to her breast. In that instant, there was a transformation in Isla. Her face brightened and she cradled the infant close.

"What do ye wish to name him?" Artair asked. He wondered if he could ever bring himself to see her as more than his brother's woman. Despite the fact she was pretty and sweet, he felt like a brother to her.

Isla's tear-filled eyes met his. "Bryce Alan Ross, after the wee one's father and mine."

Once again, Isla's expression turned vacant. "I do not want to raise him without Bryce."

His mother looked on for a long moment and then met Artair's gaze. "Would ye walk with me for a moment Son?"

They went to the garden and his mother bent to pick mint leaves to boil for Isla. She spoke without looking at him. "What are ye feeling, son?"

"As if watching a sister with her newborn," he replied honestly. "I can never be her husband properly."

She sniffed the green leaves and nodded. "I can see that in the way ye study her. I am hopeful that with time yer feelings change."

"They will not, mother," he assured. "She acts as if she doesn't expect to live long."

"I do not believe it. It is the grief and the excitement of having a child. Although she did lose a great deal of blood, I am sure she will recover fully."

"I must return to the village for a fortnight at the most. Once the new constable is installed, I will return here to live."

His mother took his arm as they continued walking. "I wished for both ye and Bryce to marry for love. Now . . ." She looked up to the window where Isla lay. "I can only pray ye and she grow to love one another."

In his heart, Artair wasn't sure it would happen. However, he would strive to be a good husband to Isla and a good father to the bairn. He'd no idea how to be either, but thankfully his father had provided a good example.

"How do ye think father fares?"

This time his mother smiled. "He seems fully recovered. I am surprised that after what has happened, he did not grow ill. I can only hope it means God will allow for him to be with us much longer."

The words were encouraging. He, too, had noticed his father had grown stronger of late. But he had been reluctant to have hope.

"Mother, please ensure Isla eats and is properly cared for by the healer. I plan to leave in the morning."

His mother met his gaze. "What of Robena? Is she well?"

At the mention of the name, he had to look away. "She is well. She received money from the sale of the Mackay home. She will not have to worry about supporting herself."

"I am glad to hear it." They were silent for a moment and Artair suspected his mother had more to say, so he waited.

"Son. Ye must allow her to be happy, to find a husband if she wishes it. I could see the love between ye and her and it breaks my heart that this had to happen." She motioned to the house. "However, everything will settle and one day, ye will be happy. I pray it."

"I am not unhappy mother," Artair assured her. "It is not what I would have wished. At the same time, I am grateful I can do this for my brother."

THE NEXT DAY, Artair returned to Taernsby fully prepared to find a man to replace the constable. He walked into the guard quarters and discovered the numbers of men there had decreased.

"Why are there fewer men?" Artair asked Struan who lay

upon his cot, arms under his head. The picture of repose.

"It seems that the Macneil's are having troubles and requested yer cousin to send men. Half of our guards went to Barra."

He searched the area, noting fewer cots were set up, and a sitting area had been returned in front of the hearth. In addition, dividers made from wood and sheets were placed between every pair of cots to give the men more privacy.

"Did Torac remain?"

"Why?" Struan asked, giving him a knowing look. "In the mood for another fight?"

Artair shook his head. "No, I have to apologize to him."

"He volunteered to go to Barra."

The statement surprised Artair. Why would Torac leave now that the way was clear for him to court Robena? Unless she'd gone as well.

Walking away from Struan, he went to find his bed. The sooner the village business was concluded, the sooner he could return to his permanent home.

KNOCKS WOKE HIM and a guard poked his head in. "The men who wish to be considered for constable have arrived."

It seemed the contenders were eager to make an impression, even to the point of waking those at the guardhouse to be seen.

"Tell them to go to the dining room and await there. It is much too early for them to be here."

The guard, whose mussed hair showed he'd been wakened by the visitors, nodded. "Aye it is rude."

Artair chuckled when the man left and despite the early

hour, sat up. There was much to do, and he had to ensure the right man was chosen.

Several village representatives would arrive later that morning to ask questions of the contenders. As far as he knew, there were three who had expressed desire for the post.

Once dressed, he went to the dining room and was met by three sets of eyes as he and several guards broke their fast.

One of them spoke. "We have been made to wait a long time. It is unacceptable."

Artair buttered his bread with care. "Ye are to be chosen by the people of the village, not me. Therefore, ye will not have anything to do until they arrive. I believe we said mid-morning."

The trio exchanged looks.

Another of the three spoke this time. "Why would they choose? It should be our laird's representative who does so."

Narrowing his eyes, Artair looked to the third man. "What do ye think?"

The man let out a breath. "I am here because they came to fetch me. I expect the laird told ye to take the people's opinions into consideration and make a choice based on it."

"Once the representatives arrive, we shall meet outside." Artair rose and walked out. In his mind he already knew who would be chosen.

A LARGE CROWD of villagers arrived. It seemed the entire village came to witness the proceedings. Among them was Robena, who seemed as eager to see about the matter, her gaze moving to where the three men stood.

The people were anxious, which was understandable after

the last constable, who'd been a horrible leader. They wanted to ensure the right man was chosen this time.

The villagers spoke loudly to each other, goading an older man forward to be their spokesperson. Artair motioned for the man to come closer, then looked to the faces of the men who wished to be constable.

Artair couldn't keep from watching Robena, her presence threatening to take all his attention. Already his breathing quickened, and he fought not to concentrate on her every move.

"Who do ye request be chosen?" Artair called out.

"Anyone but Kyle Westly. He is a man without honor," the older man replied in a strong, loud voice.

There were murmurs of agreement.

Artair looked though the faces, meeting Robena's gaze. She stood with her friend Heather, one of the woman's bairns on her hip. She was the perfect picture of a mother, beautiful, serene, and strong.

"I stand with Nathan Monroe," another person called out. Half the crowd cheered.

Artair held his hands up. "Let us hear from each man who vies for the position."

The first man to speak was Kyle. He slid a look to Artair before speaking to the crowd. It was hard to hear what he said past the jeers about his inability to keep his own wife in check, much less the village.

Artair moved to stand next to the man. "Hear him!"

The people quieted.

The man spoke about his love of the village and his wish for a peaceful life. He kept looking to a woman who faced him with hands on hips. It was she who wished to run the village, Artair surmised.

The second man was the much-liked Nathan Monroe, judging by the cheers when he stepped up. The man spoke about strength in unity and standing firm with the laird. Although a bit overindulgent in his praise of the laird, Artair did not dislike what the man said.

The last man, by the name of Malcolm Pherson, was confident and spoke with a strong voice, seeming to expect people to listen to him despite the apparent lack of support from the crowd. There was a small group which clapped loudly, cheering him on until he motioned for them to quiet. Then he told the villagers of how he would be there for them to ensure fairness.

Once the men finished speaking, Artair met with several representatives of the people. Despite Nathan Monroe being the popular choice, they chose Pherson, and Artair agreed. The announcement was made to a lukewarm response but before the people dispersed, most congratulated him.

Artair hurried to catch up with Robena. She handed the bairn to her friend and Artair walked with her toward her cottage.

"I thought ye had decided to leave," he said wishing to keep talking to her. She looked beautiful that day. Her hair hung loose down her back with only two thin braids holding the rest away from her face. She wore a rose-colored frock which complimented her complexion.

"It is best I remain here for Finn," she replied. "I do not know where I would go. If I went closer to where he is and I never find him, it could prove harder if he decides to look for me."

Artair nodded. "I agree that ye should remain here, it would be dangerous to go somewhere where you know no one. Will ye remain in yer cottage?"

"Aye. What of ye? Now that the constable is chosen, ye will leave." She met his gaze and her lips curved. "Is the bairn born yet?"

"Aye, a boy. Isla named him Bryce after my brother."

Lowering her gaze, she let out a soft sigh. "Ye are a father and husband now. It is not what ye wished. How do ye feel?"

"It is not what I planned. Fate has a way of ensuring a person fulfills their destiny, I suppose."

"I wonder what mine is," Robena pondered. "Sometimes I ask what purpose there is to remain alone for life."

He wanted to reach for her but fought every instinct to do so. "That cannot be yer destiny Robena. I am sure ye will marry again and perhaps even have a second family."

She shrugged. "We will see. Be with care." She met his eyes holding his gaze. "I wish ye well. Goodbye Artair Ross."

"I wish it were different," Artair blurted. "I cannot imagine not seeing ye. It is as if I am being torn in two. Between ye and my obligations."

"Ye are married now, Artair. I cannot accept any attentions from ye. Surely ye would not suggest an assignation just as yer wife gives birth."

"I am not sure she will ever truly be my wife."

"It matters naught."

"I am aware. It does not make it easier to accept."

Robena took his hand in both of hers. "Think about it, Artair. When ye were free, ye went away from me, not wishing for any permanence. It is not me that ye grieve for, but yer lack of freedom."

Fury made him bite back a curse. "I know myself Robena. I know what I feel. I love ye."

The statement shocked them both and for a moment, they were stunned silent.

"Ye cannot," Robena replied. "Fight to love her. To love Isla. She needs ye right now."

"And ye?" Artair said taking her shoulders. "Do ye not need me?"

Her eyes closed a single tear trailing down her right cheek and Artair felt horrible. Why was he pushing her? The need to hear her say how she felt would not change anything. More likely make them feel worse would be the result.

She leaned her forehead on his chin. "We can never be. Please go."

Cradling her face, he stared at her for a long time. "Goodbye Robena. I will never stop loving ye."

She swallowed visibly. And for one last time, he kissed her. This time their mouths clashed with the savage passion of desperation and loss.

Pushing away first, Robena gave him a long look. Then she turned and ran through the trees toward her house.

Artair covered his face with both hands and inhaled sharply at the lingering scent she'd left on his clothes and skin. He prayed the fragrance would be imprinted in his memory forever.

During the slow walk back to the village, to find his steed and return home, he allowed himself to cry. He did not brush away the tears that slid down his face, instead he welcomed the release of sorrow.

The darkness seemed to follow him as he rode away from Taernsby. There would be no reason to ever return. He was no longer a guard for Laird Ross, but a landowner who would, along with his father, take care of the people who lived on their lands.

In total, there were only ten families. Most of them farmers. It was not a lot of work, except when they had to ensure the safety of the people.

CHAPTER SIXTEEN

ONE NIGHT, A loud storm woke Artair, and he went to the window. The rain was relentless and mentally he went over if the livestock was sheltered or would need to be looked after. As soon as the sun rose, he would check. It would be a busy day.

The bed did not lure him back, so he pulled on his clothes and walked out. Isla's door was closed. It was always closed.

Despite her request that he always knock, he opened it and stepped into the room. It smelled of flowers, which his mother insisted be replaced frequently.

Isla remained melancholy, rarely speaking, and seeming to shrink further into the shadows with each passing day. Nearing the crib, he peered in and discovered the bairn was awake. The wee lad kicked its legs, demanding to be picked up.

Barely three months old and already showing Bryce's temperament. Artair smiled and lifted him from the crib. Then he wandered back to his bedchamber.

"When it storms like this it means God feels the need to water his creation," Artair murmured. The babe's hazel gaze was wide as he tried to see in the darkness. "One day ye will ride with me and we will be caught in a storm. I am sure ye will complain."

The babe cooed as if agreeing.

Artair chuckled. "Aye ye will be like yer father. He always complained but did as told."

"Give my son back to me." Isla stood at the door, her long white gown making her more like an apparition than human. "Ye should not have come into my bedchamber."

"Ye are not his only parent," Artair whispered back. "He cannot be kept in the bedchamber day and night. It is not healthy."

Isla rushed to him and grabbed the bairn, startling him so that he began to wail. "I do not want ye in my life. I do not want ye to be with my son. Bryce is his father, not ye."

"What happened?" His mother rushed into the room.

"He took my bairn," Isla screamed. "I will not allow it."

"Stop this at once," his mother stated in a firm tone. "Ye are scaring the child."

When his mother reached for the babe, Isla recoiled and ran from the room with the wailing child.

"She is not well," his mother said in a low tone. "We must speak to her parents, perhaps it would be best if she returned home until she recovers."

Isla's parents arrived the next day, their anxious expressions making it obvious they blamed whatever was wrong on Artair and his family.

Artair wanted to confront them, to ask if they were aware of Isla being weak of mind prior to the marriage. But his mother asked that he stay out of it.

When Isla came down the stairs, her empty gaze barely seemed to register the surroundings. She held the bairn close to her chest as if afraid he would be taken.

Her father met Artair's gaze. "Once she is better, I will

ensure she and the boy return. This is his place."

With that, they were gone and immediately the house felt lighter, as if the air returned and refreshed everything. Such had been the heavy effect of Isla's mental state.

"She was affected by what happened. It is not that she is mad," his mother explained. "Bryce's death and giving birth while mourning was too much for the sweet, gentle lass. Over time she will get better."

In his opinion it was doubtful, but he kept it to himself. He had much to do that day and Artair welcomed the distraction of livestock and checking on people to help with any repairs from the storm.

IT WAS LATE in the day when he returned home. Despite the heavy rain and hard winds, there were only two homes that needed repair. Most of the sheep and other animals had been found safe. The few that were missing would hopefully return on their own.

"We will ride out tomorrow and look for the lost sheep," Artair told his father, who rode alongside.

"There is something ye should be prepared for," his father replied. "Isla may never return to live with us. But the boy must. Even if ye have to take him against Isla's wishes."

"I will not take the boy by force. It could make things worse for her."

His father gave him a stern look. "She is not well enough to raise the boy, ye know it."

When they arrived at the house, a familiar pair of guards were there. Erik and Struan sat with his mother at the dining room table, each with a huge plate piled high with meat and potatoes.

Both grinned widely at seeing him.

"Ye indulge them and that is why they always show up," Artair told his mother despite being glad to see his friends.

While everyone ate, Erik explained they'd ridden from the village, and all was well. The new constable had things well in hand. He and his wife were now established in the house and often entertained villagers for dinner.

When Artair's parents went to the parlor, Artair, Erik, and Struan remained behind. Artair poured whisky. "Please stay the night. I have to ride out in the direction of the keep tomorrow and can accompany ye part of the way."

Struan met his gaze. "Robena is doing well. Saw her at the village square."

At the mention of Robena, his chest constricted. "I am glad to hear it."

Erik looked around the room. "Where is yer wife and bairn?"

AFTER HE AND the two men parted ways, Artair found himself alone for the first time in as many days. He rode to a farmer's small cottage where the family was busily repairing their roof and helped for a few hours until the job was complete.

He spotted a pair of sheep and ushered them back toward the right pasture. Then, on a whim, he turned his horse around and went to Isla's parent's home.

He dismounted then led Hagar to a short fence and tethered him. The house seemed empty, but he caught movement in the upstairs window.

No one answered the door, but sensing something was

awry, he pushed it open. Sitting in the front room was Isla's mother, face in her hands, weeping.

"What happened?"

The woman looked up, horror etched on her face. "Ye must go. Please go." She hurried to Artair and tried to push him out the door, but he didn't budge.

"Where is Isla? The bairn?"

The woman looked to the stairs. "Up there."

Artair took two steps at a time, storming through several doors before coming to a stop at one which was open.

The stench of death hit Artair so hard, he took a step back.

Isla's father stood in the middle of the room. On the bed Isla lay lifeless, blood pooled around her.

Slowly, he turned to the crib, forcing one foot in front of the other. In the bed lay the bairn, eyes closed, tiny fists up to his ears.

"He is dead as well," Isla's father, his voice hollow.

Artair lifted the child and held him against his chest. He hit the babe's back softly, gently pushing against the still warm skin.

The babe mewled weakly.

"Oh God!" Isla's father cried out, rushing to him. "He lives?"

"Aye, he felt cold because there is no heat in here," Artair snapped. "How could ye not have checked to see if he was alive?" He stopped speaking. It was obvious the man was mad with grief and did not hear him.

"I will see about the burial for her," Artair told Isla's mother when he descended the stairs. "Wash the blood so it is not noticeable she took her own life."

The woman looked to him and then to the child. Rushing to him with arms extended, she cried out. “He should be buried with her. Do not take him.”

“The bairn is alive. He will come with me. Ye need to see to Isla.”

With his precious bundle tucked against him, Artair raced home, hoping it was not too late for the child to survive.

IT RAINED THE day Isla was laid to rest next to his brother. Only her parents joined Artair and his parents. Artair looked on as the gravedigger shoveled the last of the dirt over Isla’s grave. Her parents would come stay at his house as they were in no condition to be alone, and his mother would nurse them until they recovered from their shock.

After the burial, Artair followed the carriage on horseback, his father next to him. “I should have checked on her. They left her alone in that room. It was obvious they’d only just discovered her when I arrived, and she’d been dead for at least a day.”

“Do not blame yerself,” his father replied. “She would have done it whether with us or there. Isla was gone the day Bryce died.”

CHAPTER SEVENTEEN

"YE MUST BE lonely. Ye need a man."

Robena walked faster. It wasn't the first time someone tried to have their way with her, but this man, Ethan, was relentless. She had no doubt that if given the opportunity, the consequences would be horrible.

Whirling about, she faced him, lifting a stick she usually carried in case she ran into a wild beast or an idiot man. "Go away. Leave me be."

He smiled, showing blackened teeth. "I know ye let men into yer bed. I saw ye with that guard Torac and also with the laird's cousin. Don't go pretending to be virtuous now."

When he launched at her, Robena screamed and hit him with the stick. It broke upon striking the man's lifted arm. At his cry of rage, she ran as fast as possible, but he caught up swiftly and tackled her to the ground.

"I may not be as pretty, but I will be good, I promise." His rank breath fanned over her face and she hit him in the nose as hard as she could. He pulled back, touching his face with tentative fingers.

Taking advantage of the distraction, Robena shoved him off and scrambled to her feet.

"Bitch," he called out but did not chase after her.

Heart thundering and breathing heavily, Robena hurried

inside the safety of her cottage taking care to bar both front and back door firmly.

Both legs gave way, and her hands shook so badly, she tucked them under her arms. Tears didn't fall. She refused to cry.

That idiot would not make her cry.

Something butted against the door and she almost jumped out of her skin. A bark of shaky laughter escaped when she turned to find the wayward goat peering through the window at her.

"I will feed ye in a moment," she said softly to the animal. Moments later it scratched at the door, obviously patience not being its virtue.

Robena went to the front window and looked out. There didn't seem to be anyone about. She then went to every window to reassure herself the man had gone on his way and not followed her home.

It took a while before she found the courage to go out. When she did, she continuously looked over her shoulder. After feeding and watering the goats and chickens, she went back inside and started a fire on the hearth.

It was becoming evident that she could not live there alone any longer. At least not so far from the village.

With the money from the sale of the house, she could afford to buy a small cottage in the village. And upon selling hers, there would be enough money to live on for a long time. Living in Taernsby, she would not have to worry about being accosted and no one hearing her cry out.

HER DECISION WAS further confirmed two days later when she

arrived home to find it ransacked. They'd taken some things and destroyed more.

A window was broken, all her dishes thrown and shattered. Her clothes had been stuffed onto the hearth and set on fire.

Heart in her throat, she raced up the stairs. Thankfully, there was little damage there. She reached under the table next to her bed and let out a sigh of relief that her pouch of coins had not been found. It had to be the idiot, Evan, who did it.

Slowly trudging back down the stairs, she surveyed the damage. Then she returned to the village.

AS THE SUN fell, she waited outside while the constable and another man walked through the cottage assessing what had happened.

Malcolm Pherson gave her an understanding look. "Do ye suspect who did it?"

"Aye, I think it was Ethan Fleming. He followed me home the other day and tried to . . ." She left the rest unsaid. "I managed to get away, but he was very angry."

"I will ask about and see if anyone witnessed it and speak to him as well."

She had no doubt Fleming was responsible, but how to prove the man she'd rebuffed had done it? If there were no witnesses, the constable could do nothing.

"Ye should come stay at my house. It will settle yer nerves not to be here alone tonight."

She convinced the men to help her with the goats. While they tied the goats to the back of the cart, she spread out plenty of feed for the chickens and would come back for them another day.

Once they arrived at the village, Robena guided the goats to Heather's house and explained what happened.

Her friend's face flamed with anger. "I know it was 'im. Ethan is nothing but trash. He should be whipped."

"If no one saw it and he will not confess to it, the constable cannot do anything," Robena told her friend. "I am going to have to move. I am convinced he will return if I do not."

Heather hugged her tightly. "I wish we had more room here. We can add a room for ye."

"I will find a small cottage and sell mine. For now I will stay with the constable." As grateful as she was for her friend, it was already too crowded at Heather's home.

The constable's wife Mary was an efficient sort. She quickly ensured Robena had a nightshift and somehow managed to find clothes for her to wear the next day.

The stern woman then ushered her to a small but clean bedchamber. "Make yerself at home. No need to worry about anything other than settling yer nerves." She huffed indignantly. "It is unforgiveable that a man will attack a woman without consequence."

She patted Robena's shoulder. "Get rest and do not fret. All will be well." With those instructions said, Mary walked out closing the door firmly behind.

Robena sank onto the bed. How many turns had her life taken? This last episode, though infuriating, did not upset her as much as one would expect. Instead, she saw it as another challenge to overcome. Nothing could compare to losing Finn. No pain or loss would ever be as great as losing both Finn and Artair.

Letting out a sigh, she went to the foot of the bed where

she'd placed her hastily packed bag. Inside were the personal effects that had not been damaged, her money, and Finn's tunic she'd saved.

She undressed then, after placing out her brush and hair pins on the dressing table, she went to the washstand and glided a wet cloth over her body. The water cleansed her skin and the repetitive motions soothed her mind.

The next day she'd see about finding a place to purchase and then begin the process of moving. Thankfully, her table and a pair of chairs had not been damaged, but the smell of smoke from the burning clothes would be hard to remove from her bedding, so she would have to make new.

While donning the borrowed nightshift, she let out a sigh and thought of Artair as she slipped into the bed. If only he was there. If he had not been so reluctant to remain with her, then this would not have happened. Her life would be so much easier.

Wishing did little good, so she turned to her side and began listing in her mind all that had to be done.

"This is a lost cause," Heather exclaimed for the third or fourth time. She held up a rug and sniffed it. "Ye will not be able to wash the stench from it." She peered toward the hearth. "What did he burn in there that smells so horrible?"

"I prefer not to think about it," Robena said, dragging another bunch of burned items out to the heap they'd carried from the house.

Heather dropped the rug and walked in a circle, peering

into corners. "There is not much else to be done, just to sweep the house out. Someone will be glad to purchase it from ye."

"Hopefully a man or a family. It is too far for a woman to live alone here." Robena said lifting a cage to the back of the wagon. "Are ye ready to catch the chickens?"

A few moments later, both lay on the ground laughing so hard they cried. Of the four chickens, there was only one in the cage. The rest ran around clucking loudly in protest of being chased.

"Oh my," Robena said trying her best to catch her breath. "This is much harder than I expected."

"Why are they so wild?" Heather said sitting up. "Yer chickens are unmanageable."

When a chicken neared Heather and pecked at her hair, she grabbed it, shocking the bird into a loud squawk.

Robena fell back laughing.

"Stop or I will lose my grip on the chicken. Help me get up, I cannot stand while trying to keep hold of the bird." Heather struggled to get her feet under her.

Finally, they had all four birds in the cage. The last one seeming to give up easily after seeing the others caught.

As they rode back to the village, Heather turned to her. "Are ye going to stay at the constable's again?"

"Aye, I have nowhere else to go. They have been kind to allow me to stay. Although I've never gotten to know Mary Pherson well before, she seems to like having someone to look after."

"Aye, always been that way," Heather replied. "Rarely smiles but is good to the villagers."

"Have ye seen that horrible Fleming about?" Robena asked.

"Aye, he was at the tavern the other day. I saw him walking out, barely able to walk."

She shuddered. "He told the constable I invited him to come with me and then changed my mind."

Heather made a face. "Let us think about it. Ye had offers from two strikingly handsome men and ye chose to invite a toothless waste to yer cottage?"

"Aye, I have no taste in men," Robena replied with a soft smile. "All I can do is avoid him I suppose."

At Heather's home, her husband neared and took the caged chickens. "Welcome back," he said. The birds clucked in response.

Still smiling, Robena walked through the village. There had been several empty houses after the attacks, but since the shipwreck, there were no places to be had. She would have to have one built, which could take weeks.

Instead of stopping, she continued toward the sea and sat on a rock to look out over the water. Several fishing boats bobbed nearby. Other than that, it was a quiet day.

Her mind went in so many directions, she had to take a breath. "What am I going to do?" She looked up at the sky, hoping for an answer, but none came to mind.

It would be uncomfortable to remain at the constable's for too much longer. Perhaps, she could return to the cottage while having another built. If she was careful and perhaps got a dog, it would be a bit safer.

Just then horsemen appeared, riding at a gallop toward the guard quarters. It was too late to avoid being seen, so Robena kept her gaze forward, not looking at the men who would ride right past where she sat.

"Robena?"

The voice startled her, and she whirled around to see Artair was already dismounting. He rushed to her, pulling her to her feet. When his arms came around her, she almost cried. But it was dangerous territory. And she didn't dare allow him to think it was acceptable.

Pushing away, she gave him a questioning look. "What are ye doing here?"

"I am helping track a man who stole from one of my farmers. He came this way. We came to get guards to help."

He studied her face. "I have much to tell ye."

"It is best ye do not. I—I have met someone." She turned and raced to the constable's house, unwilling to turn around and see Artair's reaction.

If he did not stay long, he had no way to find out she was not only not seeing anyone, but found herself without a home to call her own at the moment.

CHAPTER EIGHTEEN

TRACKING THE MAN proved harder than they expected. When caught stealing, the man had attacked a farmer, beating him mercilessly in front of his family.

They'd lost his trail after riding for an entire day.

Erik neared and shook his head. "No one has gone in this direction. Perhaps we should return north by another route. He couldn't have gone far."

An arrow whizzed by, impaling a tree just above Artair's head. He dove to the ground then looked over to see that Erik had done the same.

"What was that?" he asked scanning the forest for his attacker.

A second arrow narrowly missed him and he dashed behind a large boulder.

Not too far away, he caught sight of a lone man standing on the side of a hill.

"We are Laird's guardsmen. Cease at once!" Erik shouted.

The reply was a third arrow.

"Idiot!" Artair said, glancing to ensure Erik had not been struck. His friend crawled toward the archer.

"Bloody fool." Artair groaned and followed after his friend. With only swords, they could not defend against bow and arrows. Neither could they sneak up on the man who had the advantage.

"What are ye doing?" Artair whispered. "He will see ye."

Erik motioned for Artair to go in the other direction, and he understood that his friend planned for him to distract the man while he attacked. It could work.

Artair rolled behind a short bush and threw a rock at the man. It hit him square in the back as he looked for Erik.

"Augh!" the man called out, momentarily stunned. It was not long enough because he loosed several arrows, one striking Artair in the leg before Erik tackled him to the ground.

Artair cried out in agony. The excruciating pain traveled up from his leg sending him to fall back for a moment. Taking deep breaths, he managed to drag himself to sit.

Surveying the wound, he could only take deep breaths, the arrow was deeply imbedded. When he touched the arrow it was as if his entire leg was on fire. Artair fell back and pounded his fists into the ground willing the searing pain to decrease.

"I could use a hand," Erik called out, then punched the man in the face twice.

"I would if I could move," Artair replied gritting his teeth. "Would ye hurry?"

Erik glared in his direction. "It seems this idiot likes my company." There were several groans and the sounds of a fight before Erik finally neared, dragging the unconscious man.

"Very well, I forgive yer lack of assistance." He looked down at Artair. "Not sure how I can take ye both back."

Artair gave him a bland look. "Help me wrap my leg. I can ride."

The man started to come to, and Erik yanked him up to sit.

"Who are ye and why did ye attack us?"

The man spit out blood. "I am paid to keep trespassers out of my laird's lands. This is Macleod territory."

"We called out who we were, idiot," Erik gritted out.

"Ye are wearing no plaid."

He had a point. However, most of the time they never did wear the clan colors unless on official travel.

"Help me get him on the horse," Erik said pointing to Artair.

Vile curses echoed through the trees as they bound Artair's leg and helped him stand. Hagar seemed to sense his master was in pain as the animal had neared and nudged his shoulder.

"Where is my horse?" Erik asked no one in particular. He turned to his bloody opponent. "Do not move." He walked away to seek out his mount.

"Our clan is not at war with yers so far as I know. Ye should expect that most who ride by are Ross."

The man looked to him and then to the sword in his hand and sneered. "Ye should ask yer laird."

Artair would at once speak to Darach about what happened. Something seemed amiss, but he let it pass.

When Erik returned on his mount, they rode back the way they'd come. Artair had to stop several times as the horse's jostling became more and more painful.

Finally, he asked Erik to help him dismount. "Help me down. I cannot go any further."

"We can set up camp," his friend said and hurried to gather wood. Artair could not take the pain. All he wanted, in that moment, to pass out at least for a temporary reprieve.

Gauging from the length of arrow that protruded, it was

embedded halfway through his thigh. He wondered if a healer would suggest pushing it through or pulling it out? Either way damage would be done.

He let out a few short breaths and grabbed the arrow.

"Do not pull it!" Erik called, but it was too late. Artair yanked the arrow with all his might and then passed out.

When Artair came to, he lay on his tartan next to warm fire. His leg throbbed as if it, too, were ablaze.

Erik sat on his own tartan not too far away, holding a fish over the fire on a spit. "Hungry?"

"Nay," Artair shook his head. "Whisky?"

"By yer hand."

He took a draw from the wineskin, allowing the fiery liquid to flow languidly through him. "I have a fever."

"Ye are the second idiot I've the pleasure of spending time with today," came Erik's retort. "What were ye thinking? Do ye not wish to ever use that leg again?"

Artair let out short breaths and holding his leg straight, he leapt to his feet. The searing pain made him double over, but he managed a few steps to relieve himself.

"I am not sure how to get ye back to the village. Ye cannot ride." Erik studied him. "I cannot leave ye here." He looked in the direction where they'd been attacked.

"It is the same leg," Artair said absently.

"What?" Erik looked at him as if he'd gone mad.

"The same leg Hagar kicked. I finally could walk without a limp."

In the morning, Artair could barely keep his eyes open. He was ravished with fever and pain. They'd run out of whisky, but Erik promised to find some quickly. By the time they reached the outskirts of the village, Artair could barely keep from falling off the horse.

A bit later when he was helped from the horse, he was delirious. Although he was aware enough to know someone removed his clothes and he was submerged in cool water Artair could not speak or think clearly.

Voices came and went, and he could not make out any of them. All he knew was that he was safe for the time being, but whether he would live or not was still in question.

His parents could not withstand another loss so soon. They would have their grandchild to raise, but they would be mourning and once again the bairn would be bathed in the pain of those around him.

"I must . . . live."

Someone wiped his brow, and he turned his head in the direction of the cool cloth. Moments later, at least it seemed, so as he lost track of time, his leg was treated. The pain was more than he could withstand, and he considered how much he wanted to live just before losing consciousness from the pain.

When he opened his eyes again, sunlight came through the window. He was shaking with cold and realized he was nude except for a cloth across his midsection.

The window was opened to keep the room from becoming warm. Artair lifted his hand and touched his face. Cold and dry, it seemed the fever had broken.

Slowly he moved his injured leg. It ached, but not so much that he could not tolerate it. Whoever had cared for him was a good healer.

There was a knock at the door and a woman he recognized

walked through the opening. "Ye are awake," she said without inflection. "We wondered if ye would wake after the fever finally broke last night."

He searched the woman's face. "Ye are Mary, the constable's wife. Is this yer home?"

"Aye it is."

"How long did I sleep?"

She met his gaze knowingly. "Three days."

"Three days?" He looked to the window and then back to the woman. "Where is Erik?"

"He should be by shortly. He went with Robena to the market to fetch items for supper. She needed fresh air after looking after ye nonstop."

"Robena was here?"

"Aye, the poor lass is without a home. She has been living here for a fortnight."

The information sunk in. Had she lied about meeting someone? "What happened to her cottage?"

"She sold it after being attacked. My husband sent a messenger to your family about yer injury. Yer parents sent word they cannot come because of yer son but wish to be kept informed. I am sure word will be sent that ye are awake."

His son. Artair didn't correct the woman, but he never wished for the lad not to know he was Bryce Ross' son. "Thank ye."

The woman helped him dress. Each time he moved the leg, it protested with pain that shot up to his hip. Artair breathed heavily, drenched in sweat.

"The healer said the leg will take a long time to heal. The arrow pierced a portion that accounts for movement."

Artair wondered if he'd done the damage by yanking it out. He should have waited for a healer, now he would be crippled.

The constable appeared and helped him into the sitting room. While he ate a light meal of broth and bread, the man informed him of all the changes in the village.

"How do ye fare?" Malcolm asked, his gaze direct. "We wondered if ye would survive, but I was assured by your strength that ye would."

Artair nodded. "Thank ye. I do not believe my parents could have withstood another loss. I was a fool to have pulled the arrow out."

"In moments like those when crazed with pain, it is hard to make a good decision. Do not blame yerself."

When the door opened and Robena and Erik walked in, his stomach tumbled. Her expression turned to surprise upon seeing him.

"Ye are up," she said. "I am glad."

He nodded unable to come up with a response.

Erik grinned. "Just in time. I am to ride back to the keep today. I will inform yer parents and our laird."

"Let them know I will return as soon as I can ride."

"It will not be for at least a sennight," Mary Pherson added, not leaving room for argument. "Cannot very well have the laird's cousin dying because we allowed ye to go about too soon after such an injury."

Later that day, the constable went out to see about village needs and his wife excused herself. Robena stood, rubbing her hands together. "If ye do not require anything, I must see about washing clothes and linens."

"Ye were attacked."

She glanced in the direction Mary had gone. "Aye. It was nothing. I fought him off. A village drunk."

"And now ye live here."

This time Robena visibly stiffened. "For now."

"I wish to speak to ye at length about what happened." Artair met her gaze. "Isla has died."

Her eyes widened. "Oh no. What happened?"

"Melancholy, I suppose. She had no will to live after Bryce died. She took her own life."

Robena lowered to a chair. "I am so very sorry. What of the bairn?"

"He is with my parents. I plan to hire a nursemaid, but mother has asked that we wait. For now, she is enjoying caring for him. I thought after a couple of months she would tire, but she seems happy."

"The poor wee thing," Robena said with a deep sigh. "Both parents gone."

"He has me and my parents," Artair said. Adjusting in the chair made him cringe. The leg was healing, but it seemed rather slow.

"Ye limped on that same leg before," Robena said as she handed him a cup of water.

"I did not think it was noticeable," Artair replied. "I suppose when I grew tired, it was hard to keep from favoring it."

She watched him drink. "If ye do not require anything, I will go help Mary with what has to be done."

"Can we speak later?" Artair asked. He had much to share with her. Possibly ask that she return with him to his home. Would she be willing to marry him?"

"I am not sure there is anything left to say between us." Robena turned and walked away before he could say anything.

THE DOOR OPENED and the constable walked in. "Yer cousin came to find ye," Pherson informed him then continued past to give them privacy.

His youngest cousin Gideon walked in. The large man seemed to shrink the room. The dark hazel gaze traveled from his face to his leg. "Darach is worried about ye."

"I am alive," Artair replied. "Why did he send ye?"

The young warrior had changed in the time since he'd seen him last. Gideon had been assigned to the northern post for months and then had gone to visit the Macdonald clan for another half of the year.

"Ye look different," Artair observed. "Did something happen?"

Gideon's gaze moved away from his. "I came here to see about ye. Darach thinks with the loss of yer brother and yer wife, perhaps ye and yer parents would want to come stay at the keep. It is almost time for the games."

"I am sure my parents will be there. Father loves the attention he gets when dressed in full clan attire. Mother as well."

"What about ye?"

Every year, his parents went to the clan gathering and remained there for at least a month. His mother prepared for months in advance. Artair wondered absently if she'd had considered it this time.

"I will ensure my parents attend. I will try. It is expected that my leg will heal very slowly."

Pherson returned and invited Gideon to remain there for

the night. Artair wondered how many beds the home had. He recalled three, or perhaps four. He supposed if it was four there was one left.

At last meal, Gideon kept stealing glances at Robena. It was obvious he found her beautiful. When he glanced to Artair, he lifted a brow.

"Miss Robena, have ye ever attended the games at the keep?" Gideon asked, adding his alarmingly alluring smile. "I believe ye would enjoy it tremendously."

Her cheeks turned pink at Gideon's attention. "I have not. Everyone who has gone says it is an unforgettable event."

Mary Pherson took it as her cue to add her opinion. "We went once, and I am looking forward to doing so again this year." She looked at Robena. "Perhaps ye can come with us."

"I cannot. Ye know I have much to do." Robena did not meet anyone's gaze. "I will help here while ye are gone."

Gideon studied her for a moment. "Is there anything I can help with, Miss Robena?"

Her eyes met Artair's for a moment as if willing him to reply for her. Then she shook her head. "No, thank ye. I am moving closer to the village and help a friend with an egg stand several days a week at the village market."

When Gideon started to ask another question, Artair nudged his leg.

Robena stood. "I must help Mary clean up."

CHAPTER NINETEEN

"THAT IS A handsome family," Mary said as they cleaned up from the meal. "I suppose ye noticed."

It was strange that the usually stern woman would make such a comment. Robena slid a look to her. "They are. I have noticed."

"It seems Mister Artair is quite taken by ye." She lifted a bowl of dirty water and hurried to the doorway to throw it out.

What Artair thought when it came to her didn't matter. He'd only declared his love after being forced to marry. It was possible he felt that way, however prior to his brother's death, his only plan was not to be tied down.

"I have no need of a man or husband. I have enough to make my own way." Robena wrung out a wet cloth and began wiping the table surfaces. "Do ye not think that a woman should be able to live alone?"

"An old woman without options aye, but not a young beauty." Mary met her gaze. "No matter where ye live, how long before a man forces his way into yer home in the middle of the night? Ye are much too young and fetching to be without protection."

That the woman was right didn't matter. Anger filled her at the truth. She wasn't so naïve to know how men seemed to think a woman alone was ripe for the picking.

"... with all the guardsmen now living near and the lone fishermen, not to mention..." Mary continued listing the many possibilities for a man to accost her, which almost made Robena laugh at the absurdity of the conversation.

"I will certainly have bad dreams tonight," Robena said as she hung the rinsed wet cloth on one of the strings that were strung across one corner of the room for drying laundry.

Mary met Robena's gaze. "I mean well, lass. I do not wish to see ye harmed."

Her heart softened and she touched the woman's arm. "Thank ye for all ye and yer husband are doing for me. I will take heed of yer words, of course."

When she went to the front room only Gideon was there. She looked to the empty chair where Artair had been sitting. He was not well enough to walk about, so his cousin must have helped him to bed.

"He is outside and asked to speak to ye." The handsome man met her gaze for a long moment. "I am going to the guard house until he is ready to return home. Please inform the constable."

With that, he stood then winked at her. "I can see why Artair is so taken with ye."

Heat rushed to her cheeks as she walked out with him, not daring to look up. What had Artair said to him?

While Gideon informed Artair he would return in a few days, Robena studied the men. Gideon had dark hair, almost black. He wore a thick beard which covered the bottom portion of his face. It was as if he tried to detract from his beauty between the beard and long hair that often fell over his brow.

"How do ye plan to get back to yer bed?" Robena asked Artair, who was obviously uncomfortable sitting on the hard chair. "Ye should not have come out here."

"It is hard for me to remain inside for so long," he retorted. His petulant expression made him look years younger.

"With only Mary and I, we will have a hard time helping ye to yer room." She stepped inside and returned with a blanket, then moved the other chair and lifted his leg so he could rest his foot atop it.

"That hurt." Artair grimaced and shifted, attempting to get comfortable. "I have to ride back home. My parents will want to go to the games."

"Ye are not in any condition to return home as yet. Ye should wait a few days, perhaps a sennight."

She could not keep from looking at him. The man had her heart and Robena doubted she'd ever feel the same way about another.

"Will ye come with me?" Artair asked lifting his gaze to hers. "Come with me, Robena. Ye know how I feel about ye. Allow me to care for ye."

So many emotions tore through her.

"I cannot."

The words came out as a whisper. "Ye are only asking because of the change in yer circumstances. Once life settles and ye hire a nursemaid, the road will call ye back."

Artair shook his head. "My responsibilities to the land and people do not allow for it. My duty is to remain with my family."

For a moment she considered what it was like for him to have his freedom stripped in a manner that was not anyone's fault.

"Who do ye think will suffer the most for what has happened? Ye or yer parents?"

"My parents as a whole," he replied without hesitation. "My parents have lost a son; I cannot imagine their pain. I've lost my brother and it hurts, but for them, it must be tenfold."

"Ye also lost yer freedom." Robena lowered to sit on the edge of the chair where his foot rested and placed a hand on his opposite knee. "Ye must find a way to keep a portion of it despite yer responsibilities. It is who ye are."

"Is that what ye fear losing as well? Yer independence?"

The question struck her in a way she'd not expected. It was true. As much as she hated having to give up her cottage, she would fight for the right to choose her own way.

"Aye, I suppose so."

A soft smile lifted the corners of his mouth and she could not drag her gaze from it. He noticed and pinned her with a knowing look. "Ye feel strongly for me, Robena. I will wait for ye."

Before agreeing to fly to the moon with him, she got to her feet. "I'd best fetch Mary so we can try to get ye inside."

He took her hand, stopping Robena from going past. "Promise me ye will consider accepting my offer. I wish to marry ye and spend my life beside ye."

When her lungs protested, Robena realized she held her breath. She wanted nothing more than to be with him. To see him daily. However, it had to be the right moment. First, she had to be sure it was what she wanted in life and not something to accept simply because of her lack of options.

"I promise."

"He is moaning in his sleep," Mary said. "Must be in pain from his cousin taking him outside." She handed Robena a cup. "This ought to help."

She tiptoed into Artair's bedchamber and placed the candleholder and cup on a table. She then neared the bed.

His brow was scrunched as he murmured unintelligible words. When he shifted, he moaned and grimaced.

"Artair," Robena whispered, but he did not wake. Without thought, she pressed kisses to his brow, both cheeks, and then to his lips. "Shhh."

She swept hair from his wet brow.

His eyes opened and he let out a sigh. "I wish this was how I woke every day. Looking into yer eyes."

"I have a tincture for ye to drink. It will help with the pain," Robena whispered.

Reaching for her, he cradled her jaw in his palm. "Thank ye."

Once again, their lips pressed together, Robena taking the initiative. Artair responded by deepening the kiss, sliding his hand behind her head to pull her closer.

He trailed his lips across hers and down to her throat where he suckled gently. Trickles of heat traveled down her body and she clutched his shoulders to keep from falling atop him.

"Mm." The sound of her own voice startled her to realize what was happening and she gently pushed away.

"I—I best let ye sleep." She turned away then realized the cup of tincture was too far for him to reach.

"Drink from the cup." When she faced him, she found his gaze following her every move.

"Why are ye so reluctant to accept what happens between us?" Artair took the cup and swallowed its now cool contents.

Because the truth was terrifying. She could not imagine life with him and then losing him to his call of the road. She'd already lost too much and one more loss would break her beyond repair.

Robena leaned over and pressed a soft kiss to his lips. "Sleep well."

CHAPTER TWENTY

THE MIST FALLING over him did little to help Artair's mood as he rode in a carriage to his home. He'd not been aware Gideon had arranged for a mode of transport that would be more comfortable for travel. It felt odd to not be on horseback. The few times he'd ridden in a carriage had been because he'd been accompanying his mother, or another female relative.

A young man, who'd been hired by Gideon to help out at the lands until Artair was able to ride and be of assistance to his father, sat across from him.

Not only did the carriage ride annoy him, but the fact he'd not seen Robena that day before leaving did not sit well with him, either. She'd gone to the blasted market to help her friend.

The night before, she'd sat next to him after last meal and they'd discussed her situation. From what he gathered, she was to meet with the people who'd purchased her cottage—a young couple who'd been victims of the shipwreck. They were expecting a bairn and needed to move from the overcrowded cottage where they'd been living.

Robena had cut her asking price in half for them to be able to afford it. Artair doubted she'd ever collect from them from the way she described their dire circumstances.

The entire time they'd been there, the Phersons sat by,

drinking mead while discussing matters of their travel to the games, affording him and Robena no opportunity for private talk.

Apparently, Malcolm Pherson had recruited Nathan Monroe, one of the other candidates, to fill in as constable while he was gone.

It was good to know the village would be well managed by Pherson in the coming years. Artair made a mental note to tell Gideon to give his brother the news.

There had been good news. The man who'd attacked the farmer had been caught after bragging about it at the tavern. He was now imprisoned.

There was a bump in the road and he grimaced as the jostle shook his leg. His companion looked from the window to him. "I have tincture if ye require it."

"It will take a great deal of pain for me to drink more of the vile liquid." Artair blew out a breath.

The young man stared at him. "My name is Virgil Macleod."

He already knew the name, but it seemed Virgil had a need for him to know he was from the family which kept their people away from Clan Ross.

"One of yer people is who shot the arrow at me," Artair replied. "Why did ye leave yer clan?"

Virgil looked back to the passing scenery. "I had to. My father threw me out and asked to never to see me again."

Over the years, they'd heard of the clan who kept to themselves. They were extremely territorial and did not allow anyone in the large village. There was no laird there per se, more of a landowner who'd settled there many decades earlier.

"There are many rumors about yer village," Artair said. "I prefer to think the tales are exaggerations."

Virgil shrugged. "Tis not much different from the village where ye were. Not without its troubles and such."

"And yet ye had to leave?" Artair had to know more about the young man if he was to allow him to live at his family home. "Why?"

Virgil's gaze met his with a combination of challenge and vulnerability. "I will never be with a woman."

The statement made it clear that he preferred to lay with men. Artair cared not who people decided to be with. In his opinion, who others slept with was not his concern, as long as it wasn't Robena.

"If that is the sole reason yer father sent ye away, then he is a fool."

Instantly Virgil's eyes took on a sheen. He cleared his throat and resumed looking out the window.

UPON ARRIVING AT his family home, it was an excruciating ordeal to get Artair settled into a bedchamber on the first floor. Despite the passing of a few days, his leg was still tender and painful. The carriage ride had not helped.

Everyone left to give him time to get settled and for the pain to pass. Artair looked around the room, it was one normally saved for visitors. Through the open window, a cool breeze blew across bringing with it the aroma of lavender that grew not too far. He inhaled deeply, at once connected the smell to home.

He lay in the bed as he needed to rest, however, he wanted nothing more than to be outdoors and not abed like an invalid.

His mother appeared at the door with the bairn in her arms and placed him next to Artair.

"Ye cannot do much, but ye can see after the bairn while I pack." She gave him a soft smile. Apparently, she knew him well enough to guess he grew tired of being inside.

The wee lad cooed happily, kicking his legs while sucking on a tiny fist. Bryce would have been a good father. The bairn would have helped him become a better man, Artair was sure.

After the bairn fell asleep, Artair did the same and didn't wake until hearing his mother whispering to the babe.

"Have ye hired a nursemaid?" he asked.

His mother nodded. "Aye, she should be here in the morning. After I speak with her tomorrow, yer father and I will leave for the games." She gave him a worried look. "I asked Theresa to look after ye," she added, referring to the housekeeper and cook.

"I will be fine on my own." Artair slid up to sit. "I am in pain but can move about. My leg is healing."

When she left with the babe in her arms, he let out a fortifying breath. It took a few tries, but he managed to stand, putting most of the weight on his healthy leg. Standing was becoming a bit easier, but he feared it would be a long recovery before the wound healed properly.

Voices sounded and he realized Gideon was still there. Artair called out for his cousin and the warrior entered.

"I have not had the chance to ask. How are things with the guards? Is everyone doing well?" He missed being a guard and knowing what happened throughout the Isle.

Gideon lowered to a chair, his dark gaze past him to the window. "We are patrolling the northern coastline. A ship was offshore and remained for days before leaving. Then it was spotted farther west."

"Norse?"

"Why would they come here and not to the Isles north of us?" Gideon asked. "There's the matter of a group of men who are attacking small villages or landowners on our shores and leaving dead behind. It has been hard to track them as they do not have any distinguishing features and besides wear coverings over the bottom part of their faces."

Artair frowned. "Where did they do this?"

"They have no set territory, which is what makes them dangerous. The last place they struck was a landowner about a day's ride west of here."

"What do they take?"

"Coin, jewelry . . ." Gideon let out a breath. "Stupid."

"Aye it is," Artair replied, not liking that there was little he could do to help. Then again, the Ross army was large and could cover a lot of land.

"What of the men we captured in the south?"

"Put on bìrlinns and sent on their way."

"Stuart and Ewan are not speaking," Gideon mentioned, changing the subject. "Ewan accused Stuart of cheating when they competed in an archery contest at the Macdonalds."

Gideon laughed. "They ended up being disqualified for brawling."

Artair joined in his cousin's mirth while imagining Ewan and Stuart fighting. "They are too much alike and both are great archers. Although I do think Stuart edges Ewan a bit."

"I cannot wait to see what happens at the games," Gideon said, his grin wide.

His cousin studied him for a long moment. "What of the lass, Robena? Do ye plan to return for her?"

At the mention of the name, Artair let out a breath. "I am not sure what to do. First, I have to heal, and then there are my responsibilities here. I cannot be gone for long, Da needs help."

"Train the young man, Virgil. He seems intelligent and wants to be given tasks."

Artair nodded. "Aye, he seems eager. Why did ye choose him?"

"Because I can see myself in him," Gideon replied. "I am blessed to have a loving family, however, at times it is as if Darach does not give me leave to find my true way."

"Ye are a good warrior and although a rogue, ye have honor. Darach is slow to give ye leave to do what yer destiny calls because ye are the youngest."

Gideon was quiet for a bit. "I understand. But I am a man and not a child to be protected."

"That ye are." Artair met Gideon's gaze. "Would ye mind going back to the village and ensuring Robena is well? I would appreciate it."

Scratching his beard, Gideon frowned. "Aye I will, but I cannot promise it will be soon. I am on a patrol to seek out the thieves. If we go in the direction of the village, I will see about her."

"Thank ye."

CHAPTER TWENTY-ONE

"I HAVE BITTEN my tongue every day and it annoys me," Heather complained about her husband's mother while lifting a basket of carrots to set out on display. "Since my parents went to live with my brother, she's moved in and has taken over everything."

Robena could relate. Living in the same house as her late husband's mother had been the most difficult years of her life. "She does care for yer bairns which allows ye time here to be out of the house."

"Aye, for that I am thankful," her friend replied. "I do not require ye to help me as much now. That gives ye time to get settled in.

"There is not much settling to do. The cottage is tiny. It only took a few hours to put my things away." Robena chuckled. "I must admit to feeling better now that I do not have to live at the Pherson's any longer."

Heather sighed. "Mary told me they are going to the keep for the games. I wish I was able to go. I hear it is wonderful. Ye should go."

The thought had crossed her mind several times, but she was unsure. "They did invite me to ride with them there and back. I do not have the clothes or other items such as blankets to use to find a place to sleep. I cannot bear the thought of sleeping on a floor next to snoring, drunken men."

"That would be horrible, I agree," Heather said with an exaggerated shudder.

After leaving her friend, Robena went home to the tiny place she rented from a widow who'd moved to live with her daughter's family on the opposite side of the village.

It wasn't much, just a room with a hearth and another smaller one with a bed, but it was exactly what she needed.

It had been a long month since she'd last seen Artair, and she wondered how his leg had healed. Despite not accepting his offer to go with him, she'd half expected to hear from him again. He had professed to love her, after all.

She could not blame him for giving up, especially with all that he had to do. Her chest constricted and she shoved the thoughts away. It was best to look forward and not to the past because nothing could be done about it.

Spreading fabric on the tabletop, she studied it and considered where to cut to make a skirt. Just as she started to nick the fabric, knocks startled her and she looked to the door. It could be Heather needed her help and sent a lad with a message.

When she opened the door, Robena took a step back at the huge warrior filling the entire opening.

Gideon Ross' dark hazel gaze met hers then inspected the surroundings as if ensuring no one else was there.

"Miss Robena," he said by way of greeting, then motioned for her to come outside, which she appreciated. The last thing she needed were rumors that she invited men into her home unescorted.

"Is something wrong?" Robena looked up at him. The man was beauty incarnate. She'd heard rumors of his many conquests. He was a well-known rogue and yet there was something about him that put her at ease.

He shook his head. "All is well. I promised Artair to come and see about ye whenever my duties bring me near here. How fare ye?"

It was hard to swallow past the lump that formed in her throat. "I am well. How is he?"

With a lift of his broad shoulder, Gideon frowned. "Good, I suppose. I saw him about a sennight ago. His leg is better, but he has a distinct limp now. He can ride, so that is good."

"That is good," Robena replied with a smile. "Thank ye for coming to see about me."

He studied her. "My family is very important to me." It was as if he said it like a warning, but Robena wasn't sure.

"Ye are fortunate to have them and they to have ye."

"Is there anything I should say to Artair when I see him next?"

Thoughts came and went, but nothing sounded right. Robena searched for the right thing. That she loved him and wished things were different? That he filled her thoughts daily?

"Tell him I think of him often and wish him well."

If he was disappointed or impressed at her words, was impossible to tell. Gideon's expression was blank. He nodded and walked away.

When Robena returned inside, she could not keep her thoughts straight enough to go back to her sewing. Artair had sent someone to see about her. He continued to care.

As tears slipped down her face, Robena lowered to a chair. "What am I doing?" she whispered to the empty room. "What should I do?"

THE PHERSONS DIDN'T seem to mind having to take a detour to Artair's family's lands. Mary was practically cheerful at the thought of seeing his reaction when he saw Robena came to visit.

"He will be most pleased," the woman repeated.

"I hope so," Robena said. "If I cannot remain, I will continue with ye to the keep."

"Of course, his family will insist ye stay for a visit. They must be aware of how important ye are to their son. To have sent the laird's own brother to see about ye," Mary mused. "That is a true sign he considers ye important."

Robena smiled at the romanticism. She would have never thought Mary would be someone with a heart for matchmaking. "I hope so. I am very nervous about this."

When the house came into view, her stomach tumbled, and she wondered if it was a horrible idea to have come. At the same time, she'd not been able to keep from thinking about it since Gideon Ross had visited a few days earlier.

They pulled up to the front of the house and the Phersons waited in the carriage as she walked to the front door.

It was opened by a woman who wore a crisp apron over her skirts. "Can I help ye?" She peered past Robena to the carriage.

"I am here to visit Art . . . Mister Ross," Robena said, her voice barely above a whisper. "Is he here?"

The woman nodded. "Aye. Come with me."

Robena turned to the carriage. "Would it be possible for him to come to the door?"

"Very well, I will ask him." The woman turned and walked away.

Moments later, Artair appeared. He carried a bairn and had a harried look about him as he lifted the child to his shoulder and patted his back.

"What is it?" His eyes rounded as his gaze found hers. "Robena."

Letting out a breath she'd been holding, she smiled. "I came to see ye." She motioned to the carriage. "The Phersons are heading to the keep for the games and offered to bring me by."

"Aye, yes of course." He did not tear his gaze away from her face.

"Bettina," he called over his shoulder. The woman returned. "Can ye take Wee Bryce for a moment?"

"If ye would keep a nursemaid, things would be easier," the woman grumbled, good-naturedly taking the sleeping bairn.

He looked past her to the carriage. "My parents had to delay their departure. They are visiting a family nearby. They should return in time for last meal."

Artair pushed his hair back, displaying his handsome features, and grinned at her. "Allow me to greet the Phersons. Do not move."

Robena walked with him to the carriage. The few things she'd packed were there and if she was to stay, she would have to get them.

While Artair spoke to Malcolm Pherson about the state of things at the village, Mary shoved her bag at her.

"Here are yer things," she announced.

Nerves took hold as Artair thanked the couple for bringing

her by and asked that they not stop by on the way back. He would see about returning her to the village if she wished to do so.

Throat dry, all she could do was smile at the Phersons and wave. Mary gave her a knowing look then sat back, disappearing into the carriage.

It seemed as if time slowed as they watched the carriage roll away. Artair put his arm around her shoulders and pulled her close. He pressed a kiss to her temple and, once again, she was astonished at how easy it was to be with him. This time though, the familiarity of his touch was almost overwhelming, and she fought the urge to cry.

This moment was what she'd dreamt of day and night, and she leaned into him.

She took a breath. "We should talk."

"Walk with me." Placing his hand on the small of her back, he guided her to a garden. His limp was obvious, as he walked. Once there, he wrapped her in his arms, holding her close.

"Thank ye for coming. I hoped ye would and almost rode to seek ye many times." The huskiness in his voice made her throat constrict.

"I need to be honest with ye," Robena murmured, enjoying the feel of his warm throat against her forehead. "I never told ye the truth of how I feel. That I am so very much in love with ye that I cannot breathe when we are apart. I love ye dearly, Artair."

Artair tipped her face up his expression of disbelief making her smile. "Ye love me?"

For some reason, saying the words warmed her entire body. "Aye, I do love ye, Artair. More than words can express."

His mouth crashed down on hers and she almost cried with relief. Not caring that they were outside and could be seen, she clung to him and returned the kiss. Sliding his hands down her back, Artair pulled her flush against him.

To be in his arms again was a realization of endless days and night hoping for it. His body fit perfectly against hers, each place solid and firm.

"Yer leg," she said, recalling the injury. "I do not wish to hurt ye."

Instead of a reply, he kissed her again, his mouth traveling across her lips so sensually her legs threatened to give way. The familiar heat of want filled her entirely.

"We should not," Robena whispered. "Someone can see us."

His gaze was intent on hers. "Will ye stay here with me?"

"I came for a visit. I cannot remain." She was sure his parents would not be keen on the idea of her staying longer than a sennight.

Cupping her face, he pinned her with the intensity that made her shiver. "I wish for ye to stay here with me. Marry me, Robena. Say ye will marry me, Robena, I beg of ye."

A joy like she'd never felt before engulfed her and she swallowed hard to keep from sobbing. Nonetheless, tears of happiness immediately spilled down her cheeks.

"Ah-Are ye sure?" She could barely speak the words.

"I have never been as sure as I am now. I cannot bear losing ye," Artair told her in a firm voice. "Why are ye crying?"

"Because I am so very happy." Robena covered her face, allowing the tears to flow. Artair held her close, kissing her hair.

"Stop crying," he ordered. "I await yer answer," he added in a softer voice. "Do not make me cry with ye."

After wiping her face with the hem of her blouse, Robena caressed Artair's jaw. "I will marry ye, Artair Ross. I wish for nothing more than to be yer wife."

"Ha!" He rose with a loud bark of laughter and lifting Robena from the ground, whirled her around in a circle. "I am the most fortunate man alive."

WHEN ANGUS AND Iona Ross returned, they found Artair and Robena in the front parlor. Robena sat on the floor, entertaining the bairn who lay on a thick blanket.

Feeling self-conscious, Robena stood and walked to greet them. The couple greeted her warmly, but Artair's mother was exuberant.

"I am so happy ye came to visit. Mayhap, now Artair will stop moping about the house like a forlorn wee pup."

"Mother," Artair said, seeming a bit embarrassed by the comment. However, there was warmth when he looked at his mother. "Ye make me sound like a lovesick lad."

"Welcome, lass," Angus Ross said with a nod. The older man intimidated her a bit, but she sensed he was glad to see her.

Artair stood next to her and, putting his arm around her shoulders, pulled her against his side. "I have asked Robena to marry me."

Both parents looked at her in unison.

"And?" his mother prompted.

"I said yes," Robena replied, her cheeks heating.

"How delightful," Iona said, clapping. "A wedding to plan." She whirled around the house as if assessing what to do.

"Ye must remain here, Robena. We have much to plan and consider. Would ye like the wedding to be here, or at the keep? The great room at the keep is wonderous when decorated for special events such as a wedding."

Taking her hand, Iona dragged Robena from the room. "We can do it here, of course, but the Ross family has grown significantly, and it may prove a tight fit."

Robena fought to catch her breath as they hurried up the stairs where Artair's mother pulled her to a window and pointed. "There, see the building atop the hill? That is Keep Ross."

Of course, she'd been there before but had not been able to take it in from afar like now. Leaning forward, she became enthralled with the view. Roads wound up to higher grounds upon which gray walls surrounded what she'd always imagined a castle would look like.

Turrets stretched toward the clouds from which the Ross colors flapped in the wind. It was majestic.

"I recall the interior is beautiful," she said in an awed tone. "Do ye really think we can marry there?"

Iona nodded. "My husband is the laird's uncle and father figure. I am sure once Artair informs Darach, he will insist the wedding take place there. Darach and Artair are as close as brothers."

It was strange to hear her call the laird by his given name. "I have never been to an event at the keep."

"We will remedy that at once."

When they ascended the stairs, Artair and his father were behind closed doors to which Iona explained was the study.

"There is much to discuss. Several families on our lands are battling over crops and livestock. It is most annoying that people refuse to live in peace and must always bicker."

Unsure what to think, Robena followed Iona to the kitchen where they found the cook and a younger maid preparing the meal.

"Theresa, you remember Robena. She is to marry Artair shortly."

The woman smiled widely. "Ah, we needed good news." Both maids bobbed curtsies and Robena's heart skipped with happiness at being so warmly welcomed.

"Tomorrow, two women are to come see about being hired as nursemaids for wee Bryce."

Robena shook her head. "There is no need. I will take charge of his care if Artair agrees."

Artair's mother studied her for a long moment. "Very well. However, we will need someone during the wedding and right after. I imagine ye will need time alone."

"Whatever ye think is best."

Iona gave her a curious look. "Robena, this is yer home now, ye may do as ye wish for as long as ye and Artair remain. However, in my opinion, it is not healthy for a newly wedded woman to be under her husband's mother's thumb. I will encourage Artair to build another home for ye to live. I believe that is best for yer marriage."

"Thank ye," Robena exclaimed.

Robena threw her arms around Iona and the older woman

laughed. "There is no need to thank me. I lived with Angus' mother until she died."

She smirked mischievously. "It was not easy."

THE INTERIOR OF Keep Ross was just as Robena recalled. Since she was not as overwhelmed as the time before, she was able to take it in fully. Beautiful tapestries covered the walls, huge fireplaces presided at either end of the room over which crests of arms were displayed.

Tables with benches stretched over the stone floor, providing enough seating that she expected her entire village could fit inside. On each one candelabra spaced apart to give enough light during meals.

Arched doorways led to corridors which she knew led to bedchambers, kitchens, and other rooms the clan used. Upon the high board, an intricately carved table and chairs faced the room upon it two immense candelabra.

As it was midday, the only people in the room were servants, who scurried about, some sweeping, others cleaning tables. A large black dog lay in front of the hearth, sleeping soundly.

Robena sat alone in a chair facing the hearth. Upon their arrival, Artair and his parents had been pulled away for different reasons.

Just then a beautiful brunette entered. "Albie?" she called out.

The dog lifted its head and wagged its tail but did not get up.

Isobel Ross neared and met Robena's gaze. "Why are ye here alone?"

"I came with Artair," Robena said as she stood. "He said he'd return shortly. He went that way." She pointed to a corridor on the opposite side of the room. "His parents are about."

"I am happy to see ye," the woman said holding out her hand.

"I do not know if ye recall, I am Robena Mackay."

The woman smiled. "Aye, I remember ye. I came for Albie, he likes to go for walks. Do ye wish to accompany us? If I know my husband, he will keep Artair for a long time discussing clan things. Artair's mother is with my husband's mother. They see each other regularly, but one would swear they've not seen each other for months."

As they walked out and past the gates, Robena noticed that soon two guards fell in step behind them.

Isobel laughed when the dog raced ahead. "He will return with the largest branch he can find."

"Yer home is majestic," Robena said. "Do ye love living here?"

A soft smile crossed Isobel's face. "Aye, I love my life and feel fortunate to have a good husband and a beautiful son."

"Do ye miss yer home?" Robena asked, wondering if she would feel lonely for Taernsby.

"Growing up, my family and Clan Ross were allies. My mother and Darach's are childhood friends, therefore we visited often," Isobel said. She peeked over her shoulder at the guards.

"I think I may require help breaking off a piece of branch

for Albie."

"Of course, Lady Ross," the guard replied.

When Robena looked toward the woods, Albie appeared butt first, dragging what looked to be a small tree toward them.

One of the guards ran over and broke off a piece then brought it to Isobel who stopped laughing long enough to toss it so the happy dog could retrieve it.

Isobel continued. "As I was saying. My sister Beatrice and I often traveled here and the Ross' to my home. I continue to do so. I do miss it a bit, but not as much as I thought I would."

Feeling so comfortable with her, Robena suddenly wondered if she'd been much too familiar with the laird's wife.

"I am so very sorry not to have addressed ye properly, Lady Ross." Robena wanted the ground to swallow her whole. "I didn't think."

When Isobel rolled her eyes, Robena waited to be admonished in what she was sure would be a harsh tone.

"I prefer ye call me Isobel. Ye are with Artair. Am I to assume ye and he are to marry?"

Robena nodded, her pulse still racing at her lack of manners. "Aye, he asked me, and I accepted."

When Isobel threaded her arms through Robena's, she could not keep from being astounded.

"We are to be like sisters, then. Therefore, ye never have to treat me differently than ye would a sister."

At the words, Robena's throat constricted. "I have always wished for a sister."

"Ye may eat those words. Now ye have gained six sisters." Isobel held up a hand and lowered a finger for each name.

"Ella, who married my brother Evander. Beatrice, who is married to Duncan. Cait, Stuart's wife. Glynis is recently married to Caelan. Oh, and Catriona, is Ewan's wife. Every single one of them are lovely."

"I cannot wait to get to know everyone." Robena allowed herself to relax as they continued walking and Isobel threw the stick for the dog.

Suddenly, Isobel stopped and a smile curved her lips. "Ye must marry here. It has been a while since we've had a wedding at the keep."

Robena almost laughed, realizing Iona was right about the laird and his wife expecting the wedding to be held at the keep.

"I would love that."

CHAPTER TWENTY-TWO

"How do ye feel?" Artair murmured against her ear after their first kiss in front of all the people gathered in the keep's chapel.

"Wonderful," Robena replied, barely able to keep from crying yet again. The entire time they'd exchanged vows, she'd cried.

When repeating the vows, her words had been interrupted by soft sobs and hiccups. So happy was this moment that she barely cared her nose was undoubtedly bright red and her face splotched.

By the love in Artair's eyes, he didn't seem to notice. "I love ye Robena Ross."

At the words, she held her breath, doing her best not to dissolve into tears again. How was it possible to contain so much happiness without losing control of emotions? Her heart threatened to burst from joy.

"Do not cry again," he teased.

They walked out together as the people gathered cheered. Although she saw only a few familiar faces, it didn't matter. She'd gained a family by marrying Artair and for the first time in a very long time, she would not be alone.

At seeing some people from Taernsby had traveled so far for her wedding, tears threatened again. Heather and her brood, along with the Phersons, were in the great room. Several other families were also there.

"I have a gift for ye," Artair said motioning to the back of the room. "Go and see."

Unsure she could withstand anymore, she reluctantly made her way to where Artair had motioned. At first she did not recognize the man who stood by the hearth. Then suddenly she hurled herself into his arms.

"Albert," she said both laughing and crying at the same time. "Brother. I have missed you so."

His face broke into a wide smile although his eyes shined with unshed tears. "I have not seen ye since our parents' death. I am so sorry for staying away so long and everything. If I had come to see about ye, perhaps Finn would not be gone."

"Ye have family and land to tend to. I understand." Robena hugged him tightly just as Artair neared.

She turned to her new husband. "I suppose you have met."

The men exchanged a handshake. "Aye we have," Artair replied. "I have promised yer brother we will be going to visit so you can get to know his family."

When she covered her face, Artair grabbed her hands. "Ye cannot cry while dancing." He guided her to the center of the room.

Feasting, music, and toasts continued until late into the evening and Robena took it all in, not wishing to forget a single instant.

"Do ye want to prepare for bed?" Artair asked for the third or perhaps fourth time and Robena shook her head and tugged him to his feet. "I wish to dance more."

Finally, after another hour, he threw her over his shoulder

and raced from the room as the people cheered and laughed.

Robena could not believe he'd done so. Her face burned hot at Artair's obvious lack of patience to be alone.

"Everyone knows what we are going to do," she exclaimed as he closed the door behind.

He grinned at her. "It is our wedding night. Of course everyone knows what we are doing."

She turned to the door. "Isobel said ladies would help me prepare for . . ." Words failed her when he slid her blouse from her shoulders and pressed a kiss to her throat.

"I suppose it is not necessary," Robena remarked as he untied the fastenings and then pushed the garment down, exposing her breasts.

When he stooped to unfasted her skirts, Robena gasped at the intimacy of the moment. In a haze, she barely noticed her clothes pooled around her ankles when he unwrapped his kilt and yanked his tunic up over his head, exposing himself fully.

"Ye are . . ." she stopped speaking because he closed the distance between them.

"What?" Artair asked. "I am what?" The huskiness in his voice and darkening eyes took her breath.

"I had forgotten how perfect ye are," Robena finished.

Without another word, he lifted her and carried her to the bed. "I am all yers, wife."

Artair lay on his back to allow her full access to his body. Robena wasn't exactly sure what to do.

"Climb over me," he instructed, and she immediately complied, eager to touch him and become closer.

Straddling him, Robena realized she was completely and utterly exposed to him. Artair's gaze traveled from her breasts down to between her legs. Her sex constricted. His gaze alone affected her as if he touched her.

His lips curved as he reached up to cup her breasts. “Ye are so beautiful.” Taking each breast, he rubbed his hands over them, paying special attention to her nipples which hardened at his touch.

Robena leaned forward to keep her weight from his injured leg then touched his chest, loving the feel of the hard planes and angles so different from her own.

Artair’s lips curved as he caressed her sides until his hands rested on her hips. Then he closed his eyes.

Emboldened by him not watching, she trailed her palms across his chest and then down to his flat stomach. Then she slid lower so that she could press kisses where she’d touched and down the center of his body.

When he moaned, enjoying the moment, she wanted to do more, so instead of kissing, she licked a trail down to his pelvis, stopping at the dusting of hair above his sex.

He gasped when she wrapped her fingers around his hardened shaft. The soft skin slid easily as she worked her hand up and down its length, loving how Artair’s body reacted. His hips shifted and chest expanded with each harsh breath. When she pressed a kiss to the tip, his sex shifted and grew even harder.

“I cannot allow this to go on.” Artair sat up and pushing her down on the bed. “Ye will have me undone.”

He kissed her while climbing over her. “Tell me what ye want.”

“I want ye,” Robena murmured between kisses. “Now.”

Thankfully, he did not take his time, but instead spread her legs and, after taking himself in hand, guided himself to her entrance. Their gazes collided as he slowly pushed in. It was the most intimate occurrence to hold his gaze as he slid deeper.

Finally, fully seated, Artair gripped her hips and then pulled out and thrust back in. Never had she felt so overcome with sensations. Robena pushed her head back into the bedding, giving her body free rein.

Artair drove deeper with a husky moan that threatened to send her over the edge. Just the sound of his voice while their bodies were joined made every inch of skin tingle.

"Ah!" She cried out when he began moving faster, thrusting in and withdrawing in a steady rhythm that soon sent her to a secret beautiful place.

Robena reached for his bottom and dug her nails into each mound, urging him to move deeper, but when cresting threatened, she released her grip.

"I do not want this to end," she managed to say between gasps.

Artair slowed but continued moving, taking his time with each stroke.

Within moments, it was not what her body wanted, and he seemed to realize it when she arched up to meet his thrusts.

"Allow it to happen," he urged and slid his hands underneath to lift her bottom off the bed. She grasped the bedding as he drove faster and harder, their bodies colliding noisily.

She lost control, every ounce of reality leaving, then cried out as the most delicious of sensations exploded from her core all over her body. Again, and again, rivers of heat coursed through her as she thrashed, unable to control her movements.

Artair did not stop. It seemed as if he, too, lost control and could not keep from pushing on and on, each drive harder than the last, until his entire body tensed and he shuddered in release.

When he collapsed over her, he was drenched in sweat and breathing hard, his chest heaving. Robena did not move, not wishing to come fully around yet. Her body was much too sensitive to each movement.

"Mm," Artair said, licking her earlobe and delving in. "Ye are still in need."

The heat of his breath in her ear made Robena's body instantly come back to life. "I cannot possibly be," she whispered.

When he withdrew his sex, she gasped.

"Let me help ye." Artair slid down and held her thighs apart. When he licked at her core, Robena bit her bottom lip to keep from crying out.

By the time he took her entirely in his mouth, she was too undone to care if anyone heard her screams. Lights seemed to appear out of nowhere, bright and blinding as Artair suckled and sent her over the edge.

"Oh God!" Robena screamed one last time and then everything went black.

SOMETHING WARM PRESSED against her face and she turned to it. Opening her eyes, she saw Artair looking down at her.

"There ye are." He smiled widely. "I was about to sprinkle water on yer face."

"What happened?" she asked, noticing he'd pulled the blankets over them. "Did I faint?"

"Aye, in the midst of a hard release, ye stopped moving. Ye were overcome." He had the nerve to look proud of his accomplishment and Robena fought not to roll her eyes.

"It was wonderful, I do admit," she finally conceded.

"If ye give me a moment, we can see if it can happen again." He pulled her into his arms.

Moments later, Robena lay in the darkness listening to his soft snores. He'd fallen asleep.

THE BED SHIFTED and Robena's eyes flew open. Artair shifted and she studied him. He was so handsome and in slumber looked young and without care.

When his hazel gaze met hers, a surge of love filled her, and she feared her heart would burst from it.

"Did ye sleep well?" he asked sleepily.

"Aye, I did."

"Good," he rolled over her and slid her legs apart. "I promised ye more lovemaking and I failed last night."

When his hardness prodded, she adjusted herself to allow it. Within moments, he moved in and out of her in a perfect steady manner.

She gazed up at him as they made love, enjoying the way the muscles of his chest and shoulders bunched and relaxed.

It was certainly a beautiful way to begin the day.

CHAPTER TWENTY-THREE

THE LAND WAS perfect, on a slight hill which allowed views of the family home and of the valley where sheep grazed.

Robena sat on a blanket with Wee Bryce, as everyone called him, who waved a flower in his tiny, pudgy hand. He was a happy babe, rarely crying unless hungry. Despite herself, she'd fallen deeply in love with the child and knew he would help fill the void of losing Finn.

Not too far off, the sounds of hammers and such filled the air. Several of the Ross brothers had come to help build their home. Along with the huge contingency of guards, there was little doubt in her mind it would be finished in short order.

Later, when Bryce began gnawing at his fist, it was time to head to the family home before he became fussy.

"Artair!" Robena called out, waving until her husband saw her.

He hurried over, a handsome sight with his hair pulled back and kept in place with a strap of fabric. "What is it?"

"Bryce is hungry. I have to go back."

They'd come in a wagon, although his parents' house was within walking distance. It was too far to carry the bairn who grew heavier each day.

"I will take ye," he said, taking the bairn and kissing both cheeks until the boy gurgled happily.

A horse was tethered to the front of the house when they arrived, but Robena paid it no mind.

Every day someone came and went between nearby farmers, guards, or extended family.

Not only that, but Artair's mother seemed to have a constant stream of women who stopped by for a chat, to ride to the village, or invite her to a gathering. Robena wondered how Iona never seemed to run out of energy.

"I will give him to the nursemaid," Robena said. She walked through the front room to the kitchens to find the woman they'd hired and kept on after she'd shown to be so good with the wee one.

In the kitchen, Theresa was adding herbs to a pot as the nursemaid looked on. The woman stood upon seeing the babe in Robena's arms and immediately took him and left the room.

"She was fretting over it being time for him to eat," Theresa said with a chuckle. "Last meal will be simple today. Just a stew."

Robena sniffed the air. "It smells wonderful." She looked to the doorway. "Theresa, do ye think it would be considered inappropriate for me to cook once my house is built?"

"Ye will want to hire someone to help ye in the kitchen. With ye living so close to the family, they tend to stop by without notice." The woman stirred the pot then placed a lid over the bubbling stew. "Perhaps a maid to clean who can also cook when ye are busy."

"I will take yer advice." She meandered back to the front of the house, wondering what to do for the rest of the day. In truth she was not in the mood for sewing or gardening.

"Robena," Artair called from the parlor. "A moment."

He sounded different and she hurried to find out what happened. He was alone, in his hand what looked to be a message.

"My last wedding gift has finally arrived," he said with a broad grin as he held out the parchment.

"What is it?" Robena didn't reach for it. There as absolutely nothing more he could give her. "Ye have given me more than I could have ever dreamed of. I do not require anything more."

He chuckled. "What do you think this is?" He waved the parchment.

"A deed of some sort. Or some kind of letter from the king. I have no idea."

Giving in to curiosity, she took it.

At the first words, she sank into the nearest chair.

Dear Mama,

I hope ye are well. My grandmother and grandfather bought me a pony. It is much too small for me, but they will not allow me to ride a larger horse until I get bigger.

We are going to Inverness to visit the other Mackays and I look forward to it.

One day I will return to South Uist to see ye, I promise.

With love,

Finn

When she looked at Artair, there were tears in his eyes. "I wanted ye to be part of his life. I wish I could have done more."

"More?" Robena rushed to her husband and threw her arms around him. "Ye just gave me my heartbeat back. My life is complete now that I know my son promises to come and see me one day."

He closed the distance between them and embraced her. "Ye deserve so much more than I can ever give ye. Ye have settled my restless soul."

"How did ye find him?" Robena finally managed, unable to believe Finn had actually written her a letter. Her precious son had not forgotten her.

"I paid men to seek him out. From what the messenger said, it was not as hard as we expected. The Mackays were reluctant to allow Finn to write, but finally conceded. They said they would leave it up to Finn if he wishes to continue to write ye.

Holding up the letter, Robena read it again then held it against her chest. "He promises to return one day." She gasped. "Does he know where I live now? He must be able to find me."

Artair laughed. "Aye dear one, he does. I made certain they are aware ye and I are married."

"Good." She let out a long sigh. "I must put this somewhere safe."

WHEN HIS WIFE rushed up the stairs, Artair could only grin. Interesting how her happiness was tied to his. It was as if they were connected when it came to emotions.

Knocks on the door sounded and he motioned for the

maid to not worry about it. He went to the front of the house and opened the door to find a pair of warriors.

"We come for the guards who are working on the house. The ship has returned to the northern shore, along with two more," the first man said, his expression tense. "We are to ride tomorrow morning."

Artair walked out, glancing over his shoulder to ensure no one overheard. "Is there any idea who they are?"

Just as he asked, Erik rode up, his hair flying behind him like a banner. "We can leave ten men behind."

"The house exterior is almost done," Artair replied. "With ten, we can be finished promptly, and I can then hire carpenters and such for the interior."

The men rode away in the direction of the house build as he looked on.

"The meal will be ready soon. Will the men stay?" his mother asked, peering toward where the riders went.

"No. They are to head out."

AT THE TABLE, he tried hard to concentrate on the conversation. His father boasted about Virgil's accomplishments that day and the young man beamed with pride.

One of the first things Virgil had insisted upon was that Angus Ross be apprised of why he'd been ostracized from his home.

"I have a cousin who prefers the company of men," his father had replied to an astonished Artair. "Matters not to me who ye fuck," he added with a chuckle.

Virgil turned out to be a quick study and spent days with his father in the study reviewing the ledgers, and some days he rode out to visit people with Artair. Gideon had made a good decision with the young man.

"I wish to plan a gathering. I have yet to introduce Robena properly to my acquaintances," his mother said, studying his wife. "They will adore ye."

Robena's lips curved. "It would be lovely," she replied, giving Artair a knowing look as he'd already warned her his mother would attempt to take over her day-to-day activities.

"Wonderful," his mother exclaimed. "I promise to keep it as small as possible."

"Then ye will not invite an entire village?" Angus asked with a brow lifted. "Like last time."

His mother shook her head. "We had to celebrate Wee Bryce, did we not?"

"It may be a bad time to expect Darach or my other cousins to attend," Artair said.

Everyone turned to him.

"Why? What happens?" His father asked.

Letting out a breath, he tried to formulate the information in a way that would not upset his mother or Robena. "Ships have been sighted on the northern shore, not for the first time. The men came today because Darach is sending a large contingency to ensure there is no trouble."

"I will go see Darach first thing," his father said and looked to his wife. "I may be a day or two."

He then turned to Virgil. "I trust ye will do what we planned since Artair is busy with the house."

The young man nodded, his expression serious.

When Artair looked to Robena, she studied him as if seeing something different in him. Artair gave her what he thought was a reassuring smile, but her expression did not change.

"What is it?" He asked. "Ye seem troubled."

With a firm push back from the table, she stood and unsure what was to happen, he stood as well.

As was her custom, she cupped his jaw and looked at him as if he was the most precious being. It melted his heart when she did and it usually took all his power not to cry at the enormous welling of emotions which came over him.

"Why are ye troubled?" Robena asked. "Something worries ye."

"Tis nothing. I am considering what will happen. I am certain all will be well."

"Go."

He wasn't sure if she wanted him to go to bed or leave the room. "What?"

Her lips curved. "If ye promise not to die, I wish ye to go with the guard."

Behind them his mother chuckled.

"Why?" His breath caught. "Ye wish me to go away?"

Robena chuckled. "The last thing I wish is for ye to go away. I am certain that if ye remain, it will keep ye from being happy. I want to do something for ye, just as ye did for me. Go with the guard, see what happens, then return to me when ye are ready. I will be here waiting."

"Always?" He pulled her into his arms and turned in a circle. "I will not be gone long, perhaps a fortnight at most." Artair could barely contain the excitement in his tone.

"No longer, Artair Ross." Robena attempted a stern tone.

Artair looked over her shoulder to his parents who looked

on with smiles. He'd chosen the perfect bride.

"If everyone will please excuse us," Artair said, tugging Robena from the room.

"Goodness," Robena exclaimed, her cheeks bright red. But she smiled up at him with pure love in her gaze.

When they entered their bedchamber, he began to undress her.

"If I am to be away, I need to make certain to leave a fully satisfied wife."

Within moments Robena was calling out his name, lost in the passion of their lovemaking. Every sense consumed her, their bodies colliding in perfect unison.

By the time he peaked, Artair fought to breathe, so intense had the encounter been.

Chests heaving, both breathed heavily, lying next to each other, shoulder to shoulder.

"I may change my mind about ye leaving." Robena rolled to her side to look at him.

"I am considering not going anywhere," he replied with a soft chuckle.

"Ye will go and hurry back." Robena snuggled against his side. "Promise me to not go to battle."

"At the first draw of a sword, I will run and hide."

"Liar."

WHEN ARTAIR RETURNED home a pair of weeks later, he urged Hagar to gallop. At the stables, the horse was taken away and Artair practically ran to the house.

His mother looked up with a startled expression as his burst through the door. She hurried to him and hugged him tightly. "I am so very glad to see ye are in one piece."

Despite the warm welcome, his stomach sank at Robena not appearing.

"Where is my wife?"

His mother gave him a knowing look. "The house is almost finished. She hoped all would be done by the time ye returned. Robena is there."

He was back out the door before his mother could utter another word. It was not a long walk to the house, but it seemed an eternity to get there.

Despite his hurry, he stopped at seeing the house. It was perfect. How the men had accomplished so much in such little time was astounding.

There was no one outside and once he entered, he noted the front rooms were also empty. Humming sounded from the back area and he followed it.

In the newly set up kitchen, Robena stood at a long table. In front of her were several clay pots in which she was placing seeds.

When she looked up, her eyes widened and his beautiful wife rushed to him. One of the pots toppled over when she bumped the edge of the table.

"I missed ye terribly," he said, rushing to her. "I do not think I will be going anywhere for a long time."

She wrapped her arms around his neck and peered up at him. "I can breathe now." A tear slipped down her cheek, and she sniffed. "Why do I always cry?"

They kissed and held on to each other for the longest time,

needing the connection they'd been missing.

When they finally stepped apart, he looked over the room. "Are we to live here now?"

"I was just waiting for ye to return to do so," Robena said and took his hand.

"Where are we going?" Artair asked as his beautiful wife tugged him from the room.

She smiled up at him, a soft curve to her lips. "The bedroom is fully furnished."

"I must see it immediately," Artair proclaimed and, lifting his wife, hurried up the stairs.

Gideon
Fall 1604

As THE SUN set on the horizon, Gideon Ross turned to his companions and wondered if his face was as etched with exhaustion and dirt. They'd ridden all day from the southern point up the Eastern coast of South Uist, chasing a band of murderers.

A messenger had ridden from the north and delivered news that the men they sought were not to be found.

Another warrior, Erik Larsen, caught up to him, the man's blond mane hanging limp from sweat. "When are we going to accept it? They've managed to evade us again." His silvery blue gaze met Gideon's before he spat on the ground. "Bastards."

Gideon groaned deep in his throat. "Aye, I believe ye are right."

"The murderers will resurface and next time they will not be so lucky," Struan McLean remarked with a snarl. "I am sick of them getting away with killing our people."

The fact that the man, who'd sought harbor with Clan Ross just a few months ago, already considered himself part of the clan was good to hear.

Gideon motioned to a cusp of trees which would provide shelter in case it rained that night. "Let us set up camp there. Tomorrow we will reach the northern villages early in the day. We can stay there and decide what to do."

"Ian has not returned as yet," Erik stated, referring to the archer, who'd gone to speak to the laird.

The men were all expert trackers. That the killers had managed to evade them for so long meant that whoever they were had either grown up on South Uist their entire lives, or they were extremely lucky.

Gideon hoped it was the latter. If some clan members were responsible for the horrible killings, it would be hard to accept. However, he had to admit the isle was vast with many people they'd yet to meet. There were parts of the isle to the southwest and north that belonged to other clans.

"There is a large home near here," Erik said. "A family that is of Moorish decent. Have ye met them?"

"Aye once or twice. The patriarch is called Orem Aldaba, a very proud man, who has made it clear he is loyal to my brother," Gideon replied.

His eldest brother, Darach Ross, had taken over lairdship just two years earlier after their father died. It had been a happy day for the family and the clan, for his late father had ruled by fear. Gideon would be hard pressed to find a man more disliked.

"I hear the man has two daughters. The father is searching

for husbands," Erik continued.

Gideon gave him a bland look as they arrived at the place where they were to sleep. "What does that have to do with anything?"

His friend's lips curved. "Ah, so ye have not seen this man Orem's daughters. I am surprised, given yer reputation. Their beauty is said to be beyond what most men have seen."

"Moors tend to exaggerate things," Struan said with a shrug.

"It could be, but in this case, I hear it is true," Erik said.

There were eight men in total. Five decided to head back to the keep, which left Gideon, Erik, and Struan to wait for Ian to return with word from the laird.

The moon was high when Ian McConnell arrived and dismounted just and joined them where they sat around the fire.

"The laird requests that we ride north, past the villages to the other clan lands and ask to speak to the constable on his behalf."

They would be received, but Gideon doubted they'd cooperate. Nonetheless, it was worth stopping.

Undeterred, Erik continued regaling them with the stories he'd heard about the supposedly astonishingly beautiful Aldaba sisters.

At first Gideon ignored him, but the more his friend spoke, the more his curiosity was piqued.

"We can find out for ourselves if these women are as beautiful as ye say," Gideon said, meeting his friends' gazes. "We are in no hurry to reach the northern villages now."

His companions looked to him with interest.

He shrugged. "This man Orem will not turn the laird's brother away. It is our duty, after all, to ensure the murderers have not been there and caused any harm."

"So true," Erik stated. "First, we must find a loch or creek and wash up."

Struan let out a bark of laughter. "Ye think one look upon yer fair face and one of the beauties will be rendered helpless at yer feet?"

"What ye should worry about is one look at Gideon and the rest of us have no chance at getting any attention," Ian added.

Gideon rolled his eyes, though he was aware he never had any difficulty when it came to attracting women.

He'd always been fair of face; a combination of light skin and almost black hair was striking according to what he'd been told. However, the fact that he was attractive meant little because he had no plans to settle until much older.

Everyone knew beauty faded, so by the time he settled, he'd have to find other ways to attract a woman.

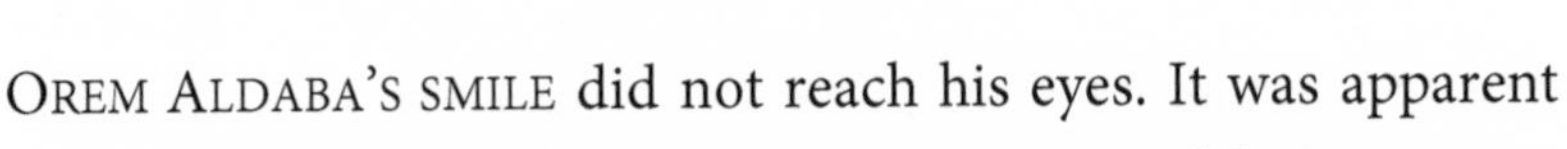

OREM ALDABA'S SMILE did not reach his eyes. It was apparent that although welcoming, he was suspicious of four warriors arriving at his home without having sent a missive first.

The man stood at the front of his house, two young men at his sides watching as Gideon dismounted.

He approached and saw the resemblance of all. "I am Gideon Ross, brother to the laird," he said by way of greeting.

Immediately the men seemed to relax.

"What brings ye?" Orem asked. The man was tall, with an authoritative air about him.

"I am on patrol; we have been hunting a group of men that killed clan's people. Are ye and yer family well?"

The man looked to his two young companions. "Aye, all is well. No one has come here to cause any problems."

He motioned to Gideon. "Please come inside and share a meal. Ye and yer companions."

It was hard not to look over his shoulder to the three men, who'd washed up at a nearby pond, expecting such an invitation.

"We do not wish to burden ye," Gideon said, meaning it. "However, if we could trouble ye for some bread and ale, we will be on our way."

"Nonsense," Orem said. He motioned the two men. "These are my sons, Abrim and Tal." The young men nodded in greeting, both seeming very friendly.

"Come in, all of ye," Orem said and the other three dismounted.

The brothers took the horses and headed away, and Gideon and his men followed Obrem inside.

He called out a name and a woman appeared. Obviously his wife, the woman was fair skinned and obviously Scottish.

"Welcome Gideon Ross, I remember meeting ye before," she said. "Yer mother was here not too long ago to visit."

They were seated in a large dining room. The house was impressive with dark wooden furnishings and thick rugs strewn throughout. Atop surfaces were lamps which had been beautifully crafted from metal and glass.

He'd never seen the style of décor, which was obviously

influenced from the patriarch's home.

At the long table, the four of them, along with Orem, were quickly served a strong flavorful tea beverage, bread, and cheese.

"My daughter Alia makes the cheeses. Everyone demands to take some home after tasting it," Orem stated with pride.

Gideon took a piece of cheese and placed it on the bread, prepared to pretend he loved it. But to his surprise, the cheese was indeed delicious. It was salty and creamy and he exchanged looks with the others, who were already taking a second piece.

"It is delicious," he conceded and grinned at the man. "May I take some with me?"

Orem laughed and called out over his shoulder. "Therese, is Alia about?"

He hoped the man did not notice his companions still in anticipation. Each of them curious to know if what Erik had said was true.

Even Gideon sat straighter to wait.

"There ye are," Orem said. "The laird's brother is impressed by the cheese and, as I foretold, has asked to take some with him as he continues on his travels."

Whether because of the sunlight that shone through the window or because he was tired, Gideon wasn't sure. What he did know was that the creature who appeared could not be real.

Rich brown waves framed a breathtakingly beautiful face. Her almond-shaped brown eyes scanned the room with curiosity, as her lips curved just enough to hint at a smile. Her skin reminded him of the hues of golden fallen leaves.

She was neither short nor tall, and the clothes she wore would be described more as robing than a dress. It did not give any hints to her body. Judging by the soft swell at her chest and the way her arms fell flat against her sides, she was slender.

"Thank ye for the compliment," she said in a husky voice. "I will ensure some is wrapped for ye to take." Her gaze fell on Gideon and she tilted her head to the side just a bit. "Do ye not remember me?"

"Ah…" He blinked, realizing he'd been gawking. "I would remember meeting ye, I believe."

She chuckled and looked at her father. "He pushed me down into a puddle when I was wee. Then raced off with my hair ribbons."

The occurrence came rushing back. It had been at the games when he'd been about ten.

"I remember," Orem said, turning to Gideon. "Ye and a group of boys had a competition to gather as many hair ribbons from lassies as ye could. Ye got quite the scolding from yer mother."

There was a clearing of throats as his companions tried not to laugh at the fact, he'd not only met the beauty before, but her memory of him was less than flattering.

Gideon smiled at Alia. "I will have to repair yer opinion of me. I believe I owe ye a ribbon."

She nodded and looked to her father. "Dalia and I are about to go see the newly born goats." After pressing a kiss to her father's temple, she walked away.

Someone kicked Gideon under the table. "I hope not to have stolen Dalia's ribbon as well."

Orem chuckled. "I do not believe so. She was a bit younger still and probably in my wife's arms."

Despite hoping to linger, after a refill of the tea and wrapped flatbread with goat meat and cheese, they went on their way.

As soon as the four got a short distance away, the men began talking about Alia's beauty and the unfortunate circumstance of Gideon having stolen something from her.

Gideon remained silent.

Alia Aldaba was indeed stunning. Strange that Orem had not mentioned anything about trying to find a suitor for her. Perhaps she was already spoken for.

The idea didn't set well. He blew out a breath. There was no reason for him to care. He did not plan to marry for at least another ten years. By them, Alia would be married and probably have an entire family.

Still. There was a way for him to see her again.

Just to bring her back a ribbon. No other reason really.

The Wildcat: Gideon's story will be releasing late Fall 2022!

Lovely story, Hildie! Thank you for entrusting me with the edits. Wishing you many sales! ~Cathy

A Note to Readers

Sign up for my newsletter and get a copy of The Hunter, Ella Ross, and Evander Macdonald's story!

I send out my newsletter monthly and keep you up to date on what story is coming next!

Sign up for my newsletter and get The Hunter Free! https://goo.gl/jLzPTA

About the Author

Enticing. Engaging. Romance.

USA Today Bestselling Author Hildie McQueen writes strong brooding alphas who meet their match in feisty brave heroines. If you like stories with a mixture of passion, drama, and humor, you will love Hildie's storytelling where love wins every single time!

A fan of all things pink, Paris, and four-legged creatures, Hildie resides in eastern Georgia, USA, with her super-hero husband Kurt and three little yappy dogs.

Join my reader group on Facebook: https://bit.ly/31YCee1
Sign up for my newsletter and get a free book!
https://goo.gl/jLzPTA
Visit her website at www.hildiemcqueen.com
Facebook: facebook.com/HildieMcQueen
Twitter: twitter.com/authorhildie
Instagram: instagram.com/hildiemcqueenwriter

Made in the USA
Columbia, SC
25 May 2022